STEELWORK

T0131414

STEELWORK

GILBERT SORRENTINO

INTRODUCTION BY
GERALD HOWARD

DALKEY ARCHIVE PRESS
CHAMPAIGN I DUBLIN I LONDON

First Published by Pantheon Books, 1970
© 1970 by Gilbert Sorrentino
Introduction © 2012 by Gerald Howard

Library of Congress Cataloging-in-Publication Data
Sorrentino, Gilbert.
        Steelwork / by Gilbert Sorrentino. — 1st Dalkey Archive Press ed.
        I. Title.
PS3569.O7S7   19921813'.54—dc20 92-9095
ISBN: 1-56478-004-X

First paperback edition, 1992
Second printing, 2012

Partially funded by grants from the National Endowment for the Arts and the
Illinois Arts Council.

Cover: design and composition by Mikhail Iliatov

Printed on permanent/durable acid-free paper and bound in the United States of
America

www.dalkeyarchive.com

to Donald Walsh

CONTENTS

INTRODUCTION

The reader of *Steelwork* whose idea of Brooklyn has been formed by its contemporary image—the borough of gentrified, hyper-literary brownstone neighborhoods, skinny-jeaned, trucker-capped, indie-rocking Williamsburg hipsters, purveyors of artisanal peanut brittle and small-batch absinthe, Lena Dunham's zeitgeist-reflecting HBO series *Girls*, the arrival, for Christ's sake, of aging British *enfant terrible* Martin Amis in Cobble Hill—is in for a bracing and perhaps startling encounter with an older, unpretty, primordial place. Whether the book's portrayal of the white ethnic enclave of Bay Ridge is any more "authentic" than the idea of Brooklyn purveyed almost daily in the lifestyle and arts pages of the *New York Times* is questionable, authenticity being a slippery concept. But as a Bay Ridge native myself and, not coincidentally, a Gilbert Sorrentino devotee, I am here to testify, swear on my mother, to *Steelwork*'s utter, total accuracy in every detail and nuance.

In the years 1935 to 1951 during which the achronological (but not, one feels, random) vignettes that comprise *Steelwork* take place, Bay Ridge was a largely Irish, Italian, German, and heavily Catholic backwater with a significant enough Norwegian population to have a park named for Leif Eriksson. Those poor deluded Lutherans aside, people identified themselves geographically by the block they lived on and the parish (Our Lady of Angels, St. Anselm's, St.

Patrick's, Our Lady of Perpetual Help) they resided in. Manhattan (always referred to as "The City"), the world capital of everything, was forty-five minutes away by subway, but special occasions aside, the various needs of this insular and resolutely working-class community were served by the diners, candy stores, churches, movie theaters, ice cream parlors, pool halls, bowling alleys, and bars— so very many bars—of the neighborhood. Outsiders, often called "fuckin' Commie Jew bastids," were suspect, the priests and nuns laid down the moral law with an iron fist and swift ruler, the double standard in gender relations reigned supreme. There were the good girls you married and the bad girls—the whores, correctly pronounced "whoo-ahs"—you slept with or tried to, bragging about it later in the gin mill. This place actually existed.

Gilbert Sorrentino was born in 1929 in Bay Ridge to an Italian father and an Irish mother. The marriage dissolved in 1939 when his father left his mother to take up with his secretary, and young Gibby (as he is called in his occasional appearances in *Steelwork*) and his mother had to move back in with her parents. That inflexible double standard branded the mother, however illogically, as a scarlet woman, one result being that Sorrentino was not allowed to enroll in his local parochial school—an early and indelible lesson in what he once called "the essential stupidity of living." He attended PS 102 and Fort Hamilton High School, and after a stint in the Army as a medic, Brooklyn College, where he majored in literature. Eventually he moved to Manhattan, working at a series of menial jobs to support his family while he wrote in the evenings, finally launching a career as one of the most original and incorruptible postwar literary figures, equally accomplished as a poet, novelist, and critic. Though conventionally and rightly pegged as an "experimental" (sorry, Gil) fiction writer, he never shed his core identity as a neighborhood guy. He remained the postmodernist you were most likely to share a boilermaker with.

I am a native of Bay Ridge, born in 1950 and educated in the local Catholic schools. In 1972 I graduated from my leafy upstate college and crash landed in my parents' house, full of the noxious delusions of superiority only majoring in English can impart and plenty unhappy to be stuck once more in my natal urban village. Then that little asshole was given a copy of *Steelwork* by a friend, and oh my, what a revelation and a rebuke. For one thing it was a shock to me that any novelist whatsoever had sprung from such unpromising asphalt.[1] For another this guy Sorrentino had rendered the raw material of my growing up—the same people I'd lived among, the same places I'd inhabited—with such acute penetration and mimetic fidelity that it delivered a well-timed blow to my college-boy callowness and a salutary lesson that it is the artist's hand, not the putative content, that creates the work of art. It permanently annealed my connection to this prickly, irreplaceable writer.

The subject of *Steelwork* is nothing less than the lives of a collation of Bay Ridge denizens as they bullshit, goldbrick, tipple, and stumble through their quotidian lives. Sexual deprivation and despair, imperfectly eased by alcohol, is a common condition, as is a generalized loneliness seldom if ever relieved by soul-to-soul communication. Work, when available, is seen not as a source of fulfillment, but rather an unfortunate necessity, making possible the procurement of the modest material requirements of life and the pursuit of that ubiquitous activity of all ages, hanging out. The theme of *Steelwork* is the relentless march of time and mutability. This neighborhood of tightly bounded insularity is threatened by change, which for some

---

1. Not that unpromising: Hubert Selby, Jr., of 68th Street between Third and Fourth Avenues and Sorrentino's boyhood friend, also hailed from Bay Ridge.

will be a release. In the opening vignette young Gibby and a friend have their ears blown open by the "[g]reat blasts of foreign air" emanating from Charlie Parker and his Re-Bop Boys' B side, "KoKo." Alien art has transformed the world: "They went outside, and the street seemed different, they saw it narrow." In the closing 1939 episode an unnamed boy (possibly also Gibby) sits alone cooking mickeys—potatoes roasted in a fire to you outlanders—in a park being uprooted to make way for the Belt Parkway linking Brooklyn to Long Island. Urban development no less than the inroads of postwar culture will transform this once closed-off community.

The thing about change is, it doesn't know when to stop. A couple of years ago I went back to Bay Ridge in search of the places so precisely notated in *Steelwork* and several other of Sorrentino's novels. In general physical terms the place has pretty much remained the one I was raised in. But the white ethnic population is by degrees either dying out or moving out, gradually being replaced by people of Asian or Middle Eastern descent. I was saddened to see that not a single one of the candy stores, ice cream parlors, and saloons lovingly mentioned in his work has survived. Of the multiple movie theaters only the Alpine still shows films; the Bay Ridge is a drug store, the Fortway a Chinese grocery, the Harbor a health club. Shockingly the Diocese of Brooklyn has all but closed down the once powerhouse parish of Our Lady of Angels, site of top-ranked CYO basketball teams and many an excellent high school dance. Even Lento's, justly famed for its thin-crust pizza, has shut down, to be replaced by the Yellow Hook Grille. (Please.) So yeah, boo hoo, Gilbert Sorrentino's Bay Ridge and mine has largely evanesced. But it lives on—does it ever—in the pages of the superb book you are about to read. Swear to God.

GERALD HOWARD, 2012

STEELWORK

KOKO

KoKo. What did that mean? Gibby and Donnie G sat listening to it for the fourth time in Donnie's room. Whole pieces of their world were being chipped off and shredded, ruthlessly. Great blasts of foreign air. A foreign air, the whole wide world entering the house.

Donnie had called Gibby in to hear it, a record he'd bought for the other side, a Don Byas ballad. And there was this Charles Parker and his Re-Bop Boys playing "KoKo." They stared at each other, sharing a Wings. They were almost frightened.

Nothing to do with the street or the neighborhood or Yodel's or Al or Eddy. Or the girls. Or the Friday night dances. The local Democratic Club. 8-Ball. A clear-edged world of turmoil and darkness. Black.

A foreign air. It might have been Rimbaud come to their ears in perfect candor. What was the drummer *doing?* The notes crammed together and released, zipping, glittering. The sound of that bright metal being flailed.

They left themselves. They came back. They laughed and played an hour of Benny Goodman and then played Parker again. The same clear joy. They went outside and the street seemed different, they saw it narrow. With people closed out from the gigantic world. It had blasted a hole in the wall around them. Through which, Apollinaire, beckoning them to his fabulous Texas. Charles Parker singing underneath the limes.

CARROLL'S
Irish Tenor

SOME HOURS after Eddy and Al left Carroll's, Frank, the night bartender, was alone with the regular crowd of beer-guzzling citizens, out for a walk with the dog and to pick up the *News*. He was a singer, sang in a weary professional vein, some vague memory of youth in Felt-man's as a waiter, singing to the customers in striped blazer and straw boater, a little soft shoe! a modified buck and wingeroo! Jesus! The foaming steins of beer with the famous Coney Island heads. That sort of professionalism, drenched forever after in some specifically Irish-American maudlin memory. I coulda been—

That patented Irish tenor. The late news droning in the background. How many men in how many small actions while they talked at Panmunjom. McCarthy was pulling the Reds out from every hole in every office. Faggots and pinkos, Joe would get em. Fuck Truman!

Frank stood at the far end of the bar, his feet spread comfortably on the duckboards, the regulars looking up from the *Inquiring Photographer* whose question was "What Do You Think of Women's Hats?" He clasped his hands in front of him, tense, so that they trembled a little: the jukebox played "On A Chinese Honeymoon" by the Mills Bros. (good niggers). Oh, the stink of the professionalism of it, the copyrighted saccharine Irish tenor pushing into the Mills Bros.' harmony.

The regulars watched and listened, smiled at Frank, at the good ole Mills Bros., at the answers to Jimmy Jemail, at the mention of Fighting Joe's stern defenses of. Frank went into his soaring solo. Coney Island raped by spicks and niggers. All the good people, the decent ones, here, now, in this bar: outside black night. Frank cut the song into dainty slivers, the ducks squeaking, only audible to his ears, his old Feltman's voice raised high, singing against all change, Al and Eddy, the fuckin greenhorn spick joo basteds. The regulars shifted their comfortable asses and waited for the world to make a false move.

What sense or clarity
of air
will sustain them
is not there.

Frank singing, in favor of all potatoes and rubbery fried eggs.

1951

SEMPER FIDELIS

RED MULVANEY came into Lento's, looking for more Reds, or pinkos at least, to beat up. Shaerbach behind him to point out the sneaky ones, or point out anybody, it didn't matter. He lurked. Red stomped and swayed and swaggered, Semper Fidelis, ta-taa! The only good Red is, ta-taa, a dead Red! Where were the fuckin Red basteds? They stood at the bar and ordered boilermakers.

We got those fuckin basteds in Henry's, right, Red? Ha-ha, Red said. Yeah. We sure got em, Artie! We got em, Red, we got em all right. Yeah, Red said. We got em. We got em good! We got em *fuckin* good, Artie said. *Fuckin*

good! FUCKIN good! Red said. Knocked em on their fuckin asses good, Red! Ha! Ha! Good! Red said. Yeah, Artie
said. Fuckin Red basteds, Red said. Yeah. Hope ta Christ
we find some more Red basteds in here, Artie said.
He lurked and leered, Red glowered and spit on the floor.

In the first booth in the back, near the end of the bar
where the two patriots stood, a Marine second lieutenant sat with his wife. He saw Red, he heard his gyrene
Parris Island Gitmo Tripoli Montezuma Guadal Belleau
Wood Frozen Chosen language and excused himself to
his wife to walk to the bar. Semper Fidelis, shape up,
cuntface bastards! You might watch your language, Marine, he said, tall and straight in front of this murderous
shanty Mick.

Red stuck out his hand. Smiled. Ah, those greenish
teeth! That corned-beef complexion. The dazed blue
eyes saw the gold bars. Shake, Lieutenant. Keep our
Honor clean, O United States Marine! O Warrior! The
lieutenant, rotten with democratic camaraderie, stuck
out his hand and Red grasped it, then swung with his
left and knocked out three of the officer's teeth. Artie did
a little dance as Red swung again on the staggering body
jerking at the end of his arm.

1942

SENATOR STREET
Miss America & Sons

DURING THE EARLY MONTHS of the war, out of some mael-
strom or strange darkness of bloody Europe, came this
family of supers, a woman and her two sons. They took
complete charge of one of the buildings in the middle
of the block, and did various ash-hauling and fire-stok-

ing jobs in other buildings, the owners of which were still too shattered by the depression to hire full-time supers.

They were, as it is said, passing strange. From eastern Europe, out from under the Nazis, or through the Nazis, somehow, or, as no one knew anything about them, perhaps simply from some dried-up Pennsylvania coal or steel town. The mother was a giant, dressed in black so old that it had that subtle green luster one sees in handled jade. Her hair was either cut short or she was bald, for no strand could be seen under the tight-fitting caplike black scarf she kept wrapped around her head. She stood always, with arms folded, after her work, a great ring of keys, for all purposes useless to the performance of her duties, dangling from one hand. On her dress, pinned high on the left breast, was a large white button with a red, white, and blue V in its center, and underneath that letter three red dots and a dash. Curving around the outer rim were the blue words FOR VICTORY. She was Miss America. Neighborhood irony. She stood in black smoke in all the kids' imaginations, her Mongol face, yellowish, without a smile to neighbor or tenant.

Nobody knew their name. It was not on their mailbox, nor in the slot over the white button on the hallway buzzer plate. Their tag therein said SUPT. A name of z's and x's.

Her older son was a lump of gnarled flesh, his arms so contorted by labor that they hung away from his sides in curves. He never spoke a word but looked about him in a dazed awe. Reverence for the ashes and clinkers he hauled, a full can in each hand, from the cellar. At times he would examine the construction of the galvanized cans, gently touching the metal with his index finger. He had a name a rush of air in his mother's mouth.

8

The younger son was called Pete, or the kids took to calling him Pete. A cheerfully brutal moron who was clearly impressed by the possibilities of his job. That is, he saw in it a Future. Advancement. He talked and joked with everybody who might someday come in the way of being helpful to him: a fledgling American, that sharp desire for success and affluence pointed in his rapidly improving vocabulary and the sloughing off of his accent. His favorite line to kids was "I getchoo inna cella an cutcha balls off." He grinned as he said this and closed one eye. But everyone was vaguely afraid of him. He seemed to hold within him a strangely alarming dullness to pain and death, as did his brother and mother. But he was quickly and surely dissembling. No one knew whether he was terrifying or funny: nor whether he was another breadwinner in the making, soon saving for a rainy day, a future uncle, appearing at Christmas, his cheap toys and whiskey breath preceding a mouth full of yellow false teeth. In ten years—he might be anybody. He might own the building. He might own all the buildings. He might hire supers, grimy with coal and sweat. Pete America, he was.

1939

BLACK TOM
Discovered Alone

TOM WAS in the corner of the cellar, behind his faded pink blanket, strung for privacy. A twenty-five-watt bulb gave off the most inadequate of light, and a cheap penny candle guttered on the old metal-topped, chipped kitchen table. He was boiling potatoes on a hot plate, stooped now, over the table, spreading margarine on bread. A day-old newspaper was open next to him. His lips worked in a play of anguished mumbling. He looked about sixty-five or seventy. He was no older than thirty.

Tom was gray. All of him. His face, though, merged into blue around his eyes and in the hollows of his cheeks: it was emaciated and pinched in a mask of stolidity. Taken all in all, he was frightening, a reminder of horror-movie monsters. He lived in Boltmann's cellar and was the heavy-labor help that Mr. Boltmann, himself merely the super, had hired out of his own hireling's pay. He gave him five dollars a week and this spot in the cellar.

Tom ate, looking at the paper—it was all nonsense. War again, the British were up to it again, the pigs, they needed to taste their blood again—they'd drag the world in. He chewed without pleasure on his mealy, soggy potatoes. Then he sat back and lit an almost burnt-out corncob. He'd write the letter tomorrow night, they could wait another day or so, there, in the damp greenness of it. Soon, he'd send for them, the depression was lifting, breaking, he could feel that, just this past month he'd had almost more handyman jobs, odd jobs, than he could handle—and he was taking out, now, ashes for three more buildings at a dollar a building—three dollars more a week. The passage from Ireland wouldn't be that much trouble—in a few years she'd be here, with the boy. Who was almost six now.

He puffed at the pipe, inhaling wisps of the Granger. A sudden gloom came down and throttled him and he began to sob. Nothing would end, ever, they'd never come over, he'd never go back. He stood up, sobbing, stripped his gray work shirt off and changed into a gray-white dress shirt. He would get to the Novena and feel better. The potatoes were iron, bitter clumps of pig iron in his stomach. He heard his own voice in his mind, saying Mary. The sun threw his shadow on the wooden floor. She was stirring the coals in the stove. He blew out the candle, put on his coat, and turned the light off, walked surely through the abrupt darkness to the door and out into the cool air of the cellarway. He heard children playing on the street in the soft twilight, and began walking fast, gathering momentum so that he could rush up the stairs and out among them, through them, past them, avoiding, perhaps, their fearful taunts and screeches. Black Tom! Black Tom! He'll getcha down the cellar an cut off yer arm! Lookout, it's Frankenstein, one said as he emerged. Gray, gray, part and parcel of the gathering darkness.

1941

THE METZES

HE WAS an old man, bald, always wore a cap. He walked duck-footed, painfully, in worn slippers. His wife was at least a head taller, a hawkfaced harridan, with the same walk, but she could move swiftly. They were the supers for two buildings in the middle of Senator Street.

It was the delight—it was the need for the boys on the block to torment them. The Metzes took a proprietary interest in the property, and if a boy who didn't live in either building so much as leaned against the wall, old Charlie Metz would come out the door, shuffling in his slippers, toward him. He would wave his hand and make a guttural sound. He rarely spoke and when he did it was always to say "damn kid" or "damn so'bitch"—but mostly it was grunts. Mrs. Metz occasionally joined him and then the offenders would have to run. When Charlie came alone they'd stay just out of his reach, dancing around, giving him the finger, clapping their hands.

If the Metzes sometimes ignored them, they became loud. If they continued to ignore them, they became louder. They threw garbage at the old man and his wife. They spit in the halls. They ran into the halls and screamed at the top of their lungs, until they saw the ground-floor apartment door open, and they'd flee. They tore up newspapers and scattered them on the street in front of the buildings, spilled ink on the pavement, drew giant leering faces in chalk on the concrete walls.

To be cruel, crueler. Don't give them a break. Annoy them and harass them—it was necessity. The Metzes were insane in their care of these damn old houses. They would be insane in their protest.

They squirted lighter fluid on the Metzes' windowsill one night, and put a match to it. The window burst into great sheets of orange flame, the glass itself seemed to be on fire.

Old Charlie came out in his slippers and a bathrobe, his wife behind him, struggling into her robe, her flabby breasts swinging beneath the cotton nightgown. They were terrified, old Charlie gibbering and his eyes staring at the dark. She held him with great tenderness around the waist, almost rocking him back and forth, propelling him away from the window, the flames out now.

The boys stood across the street and stared at them. They were so old and ugly and pathetic. They were so vulnerable. But they scared the fuckin asses off them. Fuck em and their houses. The old duck-footed basteds! The old couple shivered in the winter night. Let em get back in the house, the old basteds, before they freeze to death.

Maybe they come *out* to get warm! Laughter. Genuine laughter.

QUEEN OF WANDS

Mrs. Elkstrom was Swedish and came, years before, from some pine-dark village set between cold lakes. She spoke with a heavy accent, in that clear singsong vulgar comedians parodied. She lived in the rear first-floor apartment in the same house the Glades lived in and was friendly with everyone. Her face was skull-like and emaciated, but the children loved her. She gave soup to the neighbors, her own soup, that was magnificent. Vegetable, bean, pumpkin. Fruit soups that were spiced and aromatic.

She had seen her son in her mind's eye drown one day on a canoeing trip he had taken when she was a young wife and mother in Sweden. The slender body, pitched out of the canoe and dragged under by the currents. She had the gift of clairvoyance and could foretell the future. She knew the zodiac and drew charts at the kitchen table filled with strange signs and symbols, numerals, the calendar open before her. At Christmas she made sweet potatoes whipped with melted marshmallows.

Her husband was a heavy drinker, an ex-sea captain who now painted bridges, his legs twisted and bowed from a terrific fall he had once taken. He had white hair and a clear, boyish face and could speak very little English. His wife's magic powers awed him and he believed in them implicitly. She could read the cards and tea leaves, and spoke of the Jacks as Knaves. She couldn't play any card games, not even gin, for she saw in the simplest formalities of the games hazy prognostications.

He never drank at home, not that she would not have allowed it or even frowned on it, but he maintained a sharp respect for her area. Except that during the holidays he would make glug on the stove, great pots of it, mixing and stirring the liquors and wines, the cloves and sugar and cinnamon, the oranges and lemons. Everybody would be invited in for a glass. It was elixir, a nectar, the fumes alone enough to intoxicate nondrinkers.

She told the weather from the flight patterns of sparrows in the sky. The color of the sunset. She cured infections by placing the skin of an egg or a piece of wet bread over the inflammation to draw the poison out. And made dark salves out of leaves she gathered in the park. She prayed to God but would not go to church. Her daughter was a slut who went out to Hollywood to live with a bit-actor in Westerns. She had seen that journey in the cards when the girl was five.

All the neighbors went to her funeral. Her husband shipped out again as chief mate on a coastal tanker. Too good for the greasy scow, he called it. But there was nothing to come home to. The aroma of fresh vegetables and stock. Slap of the soft, worn cards.

1942

THE VIKINGS

WERE FOUR. Warren, Ivan, Roy, and Red. Up to this time they were just kids, but some strange magic was worked somehow and they discovered that they were blood brothers. Or cousins. Or they had families that came from the same towns, the same fishy rites and barbaric drinks. Hot liquors to guard against the northern lights.

Blood of the Laplanders, Esquimaux, gnawing on enormous reindeer shanks, raw meat and bloody bones.

Perhaps it was the war that so brought them together, some twisted Americanization of Aryan power and sublimity. Or that their fathers were all superintendents who hired bums and immigrants to do all their work for them. Fake landlords. They banded together. Comrades in arms, asshole buddies.

They marched in the park on Leif Erickson Day and ate ice cream in the Lutheran church. They made fun of Dolores' big nose and tormented Duck over his passion for her. And he was almost a Norwegian! That was unforgivable.

They had the aura of corn and wheat fields about them though they had all been born in the neighborhood. They looked to go to sea. And discover America? They marched for Brave Leif and Eric the Red, crushed against glowing girls in their musty native costumes. They got drunk like men. Even dirty and sweaty they shone.

Although they were only average ball players they grouped together and dominated every game. If they couldn't all play on the same side none would play. They tortured Sprenger for his blind adoration of Lizzie. Cruelly. And started a vogue, a whole style of harassment that persisted. They were geniuses of the banal. They joined the same Boy Scout troop, one that met in the basement of a Norwegian Baptist church, and quit together because there were too many Italians in it.

They said hello to Cockroach Malone and chatted with him. They were inattentive at school and passed everything painfully, but passed everything. At the Teen Canteen dances on Friday nights they clustered together in their drape suits, looking for blondes.

The rest of the boys still thought of them as individuals, so that they were ignorant of this configuration of power and loyalty. Suddenly they were a gang and directed the activities of the block. Everyone played their games, when and where they wanted them played. They ran things, they decided on movies to see, what not to see. Threw slush at Sprenger in the winter. Wanted cars and talked about flying airliners and joining the submarine service.

Spoke snatches of garbled Norwegian and ate lutefiske and lingonberries. Fell in love with Doris Day. The avant-garde of America come, in strange guise, to the neighborhood.

1941

TO ARMS
McGinn

ON PEARL HARBOR DAY, McGinn heard the news of the attack playing touch football in the playground. The Japanese had done it! There they were out there. Far away. He didn't quite know what they looked like but they had big swords and shit like that. Rising Sun? They tortured the Chinese a lot. He remembered the War cards he had collected for years.

Naked Chinese charging across a bridge against machine guns. The card's dominant color was red, for the blood. All the cards had a lot of red in them. Severed heads, children in Barcelona? with ragged holes where their eyes should be. A lot of crazy jigs in the desert throwing spears at Italian planes. Let the boogies an wops kill each other, Cockroach once told him.

Now America was in it. He'd get to go in, too. Get the fuck away from here an kill some fuckin Japs. Or somebody. He was sixteen and could easy make it. The war wouldn't end so quick.

They were out there. They sneaked in, the yella bast-
eds, right in an bombed the shit outa all the ships, on
Sunday! Sunday! They got no rules, rape kids an nuns.
There were nuns on the War cards. He thought of Sister
Margaret Mary, dirty little basteds running after her.
He stood in front of them an kicked their balls off! The
rat fucks.

Maybe he could even get in now. School was a mystery to him and his grandma might be able to sign a
paper or something. Get to be a pilot and bomb the ass
off them, with a scarf. Plenty of snatch back on leave.
You could fly off a carrier.

He started to run to Yodel's where he could talk about
it. Jesus Christ! A fuckin war!

1939

McGINN
Screaming for Grandma

GIBBY WALKED into the hall, too late, again, to turn
around and run out, though that's what he wanted more
than anything else to do. McGinn pounding on the apartment door, at the end of the ground-floor hallway.
Grandma! Grandma! He was screaming it, pounding the
door so hard that it shook on the frame. Gibby scooted
past him and up the stairs, feeling McGinn's eyes in his
back, although McGinn hadn't even noticed him,
wrapped in fury at his absent grandmother.

Gibby had seen him doing this once before, walking
in on him like this, and that time, McGinn had turned
to look at him, his arms still raised on either side of his
head, his eyes seemed specifically enraged, at him, now,

with the grandmother not there to be bullied. He seemed, too, so big to Gibby, fourteen years old. He had watched him play ball in the streets with Fat Parez, Pep, Buddy, all the giants.

McGinn had said you little shitface to him. Then pounded the door again, screaming, Grandmaaaaa-a-a-a-a-a! Although later he found out that McGinn knew his grandmother would probably be out at that time. A month later, he found them together in the hall, McGinn crying hysterically, his grandmother stroking his hair. Gibby had to snake around them to start up the stairs, though neither of them took any notice of him.

For months, he thought of that door as McGinn's possession. A strange and spooky door, even after the grandmother had died, and McGinn had gone a few blocks away to live with an aunt. He saw him occasionally, in his blue knickers and white shirt, his blue knitted tie, coming out of Our Lady of Angels Parochial School. He'd be swinging his heavy, scarred schoolbag at other kids' heads, or knocking the books out of their hands.

Once, in some small and unintended display of weakness, he ran up to Pep and asked him if he was going to the Alpine to see the swell new Foreign Legion picture, Beeoo Gesty.

1939

THE MOVIES

THE KIDS would hustle for the money starting at about eight on Saturday morning so that they could be on line at eleven thirty. Steal from newsstands, carry packages home from the stores, help wash cars—anything. Get that eleven cents up. The line would be long. Hundreds of screaming kids, jumping, bucking the line, everybody had a friend who was holding his place—They just left, They were there all the time. Fuck you! There were Dick Tracy badges, and Daredevils of the Red Circle cards, all sorts of things.The kids read their numbers against the numbers on the sign in front to see if they could get in free. They stood in rain and snow and stunning heat, checked their numbers, gave each other hotfoots, shoved and yelled. Free bags of candy, stale sourballs, a stick of rock-hard gum, a lollypop and maybe a marshmallow twist, rubberlike. Sometimes a free creamsicle, a comic book with the cover ripped off, anything, get em in! A double feature, five cartoons, coming attractions, a Pete Smith specialty, a Robert Benchley short, a travelogue *Wondrous Waves of Waikiki,* some theaters a race, the winning ticket got a bicycle, a pair of roller skates, an Erector set. Everybody knew this had to be fixed, nobody ever knew the winners or anyone who had ever heard of the winners. Bags full of water off the balcony, condoms blown up and floated, the horrendous din of the children, the fights, the scrambling in the aisles, the leaping through the dark, up and down the theater. Howls at the movies shown, hisses. Clap for the bad guys in the serials, magnificent bravado. Hiding behind the seats in *Dracula* and *The Wolf Man.* Smoking in the men's room, smoking in the rows, passing the butt back and forth, Fuck the matron! Here comes the matron! Ah, *fuck* the matron! Feeling up girls, necking, everybody knew a story about some girl who got fucked right in the aisle in the Electra, or the Stanley. You got bedbug bites in the Stanley. They held out on the free candy in the Sunset one Saturday because there were too many kids. Then they threw it to mobs of them out in the streets, the goddam manager was sweating they were gonna tear the goddam theater down. The armrests torn out of the back row of seats in the Electra so you could lie down on them. Everybody knew about the guys who got blown in the Bay Ridge. That was a fuckin whorehouse. They ran across the stage, giant shadows on the screen, some of them stopped in front of the monstrous figures of Spencer Tracy and Clark Gable and mugged and the place roared. They blew up their empty candy bags and exploded them in the love scenes. The girls said SHH. The few adults insane enough to be in the theater complained to the manager for three hours and then left. Those who couldn't raise the money got in through the fire doors in the alleys with a can opener. The doors would open and the place would flood with light, the ushers rushing down toward the open doors and kids streaming in, diving under seats, running up and down aisles, sitting down so swiftly into a relaxed position they looked as if they'd been there all day. See the first feature again, see the second feature, walk up and down looking for friends, guys yelling into the ears of a couple who thought they'd found a quiet spot. Who's that guy? He's in every movie! It was Franklin Pangborn, it was Eugene Pallette, it was Jimmy Gleason, it was Charlie Ruggles, it was Edward Everett Horton, it was Arthur Treacher. When they got out it was supper time. Next week *Door of Doom,* the basted'll fall right in a haystack.

SPRENGER
Butterfly Kisses

GIBBY SAW the motorbike parked outside of the Strauss Store on Fifth and did a quick about-face, but before he could make it back to the corner, Sprenger came out of the store and saw him. He had a package in his hand and waved it at Gibby's back, calling him. For a second, Gibby thought of running, but stopped and turned, then slowly walked back to him. Haven't seen you for a while, Spreng—been traveling? Down to Wilmington once or twice, Sprenger said. No big deal—went down to see my aunt. Jesus, it's good to see *you.* He fidgeted with the package. Ya wanna beer? I see Henry's is open by now —come on, I got a few bucks.

I gotta go see my mother, Gibby said. I mean, she's not feeling well. I gotta see if she wants me to go to the store or anything. He was looking at Sprenger, the stubbly beard, the sky blue, clean, and open behind his head. He looked like a drunk. One beer, Sprenger said.

That crazy party, Sprenger said. They were in Henry's, sitting at the far side of the bar, away from the door. Gibby was working on his third boilermaker. What the hell, he figured. Sprenger. Now the party. He drank the rye and lit a cigarette. Oh that was some crazy party! Sprenger said. Christ, I threw my pants an fuckin shoes out the window, every goddam thing. You were drunk, you were drunk, no? Gibby said. Then he remembered that he wasn't drunk, that *he* was drunk and Kenny—

and some weird cousin or nephew or something was drunk, but Sprenger was just—the sword! The sword. He sliced a painting in two? Did you fuck up a painting that night? I mighta fucked up anything. Don't you remember that letter? Don't you remember the—*occasion* for the party? This girl that I was going with, she type-writed this letter to—

Well, Gibby said. Well, well. Well-o-well. It was his sixth boilermaker. The rye tasted simply saccharine. I gotta go after this one, my mother, the shopping. Ya know my grandfather's been sick. Jesus, Sprenger said. Ya know, I always liked your grandfather, no bullshit about him atall—a real nice guy, a nice old guy. Jesus, I remember him every night in the summertime goin for his can a beer. Summertime, wintertime, Gibby said. Spring an fall—he don't fuck around, my grandfather. He likes his brew. Gibby drained his glass. Outside, the blue had become gray, cloudy. It looked like snow. I always liked that old man, Sprenger said. Been sick, hah? I always liked him.

Oh yeah, it was a great party. I was drunk, so I just about remember you were throwing things out the win-dow—you broke the window? Screams of anguish. Re-criminations. Down with womankind. You were very—wrought up. He was drinking only beer now, trying to stay reasonably sober, for some reason.

Oh yes, Christ. She was worth all the time I give her, Sprenger said. Christ, on the way down to Wilmington this last time I kept thinkin about her an those butterfly kisses she used ta give me—you know. He blinked his eyes rapidly—with her fuckin eyes right up against ya cheek. Jesus—I told you about that three, four years ago. We sat in some joint, I think we had a coupla drinks, like now—Cokes you drink, Gibby said, like now. You got some hardon for Cokes, kid—I like em, Sprenger said.

We were somewhere, he said. Maybe it was coffee,

an I tole you about the butterfly kisses.

Not me, Gibby said. I never heard of butterfly kisses
—the important thing is did she give you some butterfly
fingers, like in your fly? Butterfly kisses—not me. I
coulda sworn it was you. The lonely road has got to you,
old knight-errant.

It was snowing when they left Henry's, calm and
quiet, no wind at all, the huge flakes falling wet. I gotta
really go, Spreng, Gibby said. Listen, Sprenger said. Give
my regards to your mother. Yeah, Gibby said. He started
down the street, he'd cut down 69th to Third, get to the
Melody Room and keep the drunk going. An your grandfather! Jesus! I'm really sorry to hear that! For Christ's
sake, Gibby thought, angered. Helpless in it. For Christ
sake! he shouted, turning around to Sprenger, walking
backward. He's not *dead!* Sprenger was waving the
package at him, a scarecrow.

1946

TYPEWRITED
The Letter to Sprenger

DEAR EDGAR,

I've thought and thought about this letter to you
til I'm allmost sick. And I hate to do it, but though I've
wracked my brain I can't see any other way altho I know
that you will think this is pretty mean and low. What I
mean is that between you and I we shouldn't see each
other any more at all period. Not even for a walk and go
to a dance once in a while. Because we must consider
our Religius diferences. Don't you think?

I know that my Mother and Father and your Parents too if you'd be honest with me really want the best for us both so I think we should connsider them and break up before we get too serious. This is just as hard for me as it is for you onely you probably won't think so.

The Miracleous Medal I gave you you are free to keep and I wish you would because Mary is always sure to intersede with Jesus Her Son if you pray first, to her. And it would be a Remembrance, like a Suoveneir from me.

I want to assure you that it was really a lot of fun and good times Edgar and I think you are really a teriffic young man and I hope you meet some really nice and fine girl of your own Religiun.

Very truly yours,
Irene

1946

SPRENGER
Butterfly Kisses

UNEXPECTEDLY, Donnie G met him on the street one day, up near Eighth Avenue. Come on, Donnie, I'll buy ya a hot chocolate. It was early March, bitter northeastern clouds flat over all the sky. Donnie didn't want to stick around Sprenger, but there was really no way out. They went to an ice cream parlor nearby and sat in the back. It was empty and quiet.

Butterfly kisses, Sprenger said later. That's what she always gives me, like this. He leaned over toward Donnie's face and tried to press his cheek against Donnie's, rapidly blinking his eyes as he did so. Get the fuck outa here, Donnie said. Come on, get the fuck away!

So you have got a girl, Donnie said, working on a second cup of hot chocolate. I kinda thought maybe you did, you never come around. Yeah, Sprenger said. I met her at a dance, just went to a dance one night by myself and there she was an we left together, and . . . he snapped his fingers. Some pig she must be, Donnie G thought.

When she does that though, with her eyes—her eye-*lashes,* I mean . . . Jesus! I never felt anything like that! She's so soft an she smells so good—oh not perfume or anything, clean. Donnie imagined the smell of Sprenger's feet in the summertime, or in a warm room—the back of Yodel's in winter, with everybody close in a booth and Sprenger's foot smell like fresh shit.

Serious? he said. I doan know, Sprenger said. I doan know. I know that she understands me, and she likes me. She gave me this. He reached in his pocket and dug for a minute, then pulled his hand out and spread it in front of Donnie. It was a Miraculous Medal, Mary in silver bas-relief against an azure background. You ain't Catholic, Donnie said, are you? No, Sprenger said, but she is. An she gave me this medal—that's a little serious, I think, doncha think so?

Sprenger was munching on one of the Social Teas that came with his hot chocolate. He had dunked it and a stream of the chocolate ran light-brown down his chin. He sucked at the corner of his mouth, then rubbed at his chin with the back of a forefinger.

Sometimes I get so raunchy, I . . . I mean we're on her porch, in the dark, she lives on Fort Hamilton Parkway in a two-family house, we're on her porch an she's givin me the butterfly kisses an I have to back away a little bit, you know, my cock is stickin out so stiff I don't want her to feel it. Jeez!

So are you comin around at all any more? Are we gonna see you before you get married? They were outside now, walking toward the park. Donnie didn't care one way or the other, bundling into his collar against the beginning snow.

1945

THE LOVER

KENNY KISSED HIS ARM, in the dark. The muscatel sweet and whirling in his head. He kissed his arm, hugged himself. The taste and odor of her. He licked the tender skin in the crook of his elbow. The feel of her delicate fingers on his back. The feel of his back to her slender fingers.

Well, this is Friday night. You know what you can do with Friday night, right? Well, you can fuck Friday night! He drank some more wine and held the bottle up toward the glow from the lamppost down on the path, then settled himself down into the grass, in absolute misery. Alone in the park. Friday night. You know what you can do with it? You can fuck it!

Monday morning he would be back in school, to look at her, feel that sweet pain, die for her all over again, a death every minute. He kissed his wrist and spoke to himself with her voice. He replied to her with his. Strong and sure, grateful but clearly in control. I've loved you all these months, she was saying. Her voice soft and perfumed in the quiet darkness. All these months, she said. How couldn't you see it? I could have died when you passed by me every day. But, he said. But,

I thought you didn't care about me at all. You were always with your friends, laughing. You didn't know anybody I knew. Her breath, turned and mixed with his. The smell of soap from her. Sensed her thighs beneath her skirt.

She's with some guy right now! Some goddam basketball player, at some goddam dance! Or a sailor or some goddam Marine with all his fancy shit uniform shit on. He lay down and cradled his head in his arms, licked the grass and tasted her. He wanted to die. Tears came into his eyes.

Monday soon and he would see her. He'd talk to her, just talk to her, walk up to her in the cafeteria and ask her to go out with him. Let her silly fuckin girlfriends laugh all they want. Maybe she liked him anyway. How could you pass me by every day, she said, he whispered. He placed his head so that his voice was soft, trapped in the grass and coming to his ears as hers. My dear, he said. My dear, my dear, my dearest. He began to cry. He writhed around on the grass and reached out for the muscatel. I can't stand this, he said aloud. How could he live through the weekend? He couldn't eat. Why should she do this to him? He was minding his own business. He didn't ask to see her. He wanted to die rather than face the weekend without her and thinking of her. My love, she said.

She was naked, a honey-colored down on her thighs, darker hair sweet between her legs. Her eyes were shining. Oh God. He rolled around on the grass, grinding his teeth, clutching the bottle to his chest. They were tender virgins together, fumbling into love. He kissed her fingers and palms, bit her earlobes. She breathed quietly, her eyes half-closed, smiling. Her white teeth. Oh God.

To be in her. What would it be like to be in her? What does that feel like? Taken in and held by her, God, warm and wet, so close. His tongue in her mouth at the same time, whispering and groaning against her wet lips. She doesn't care. I don't want to . . . fuck her anyway. Just touch her. I just want to touch her. To kiss her. I'm not just horny. Her wet lips. To kiss her ears. To brush her hair for her. To be alone with her on Sunday afternoons.

Monday she wore a brown suit and a yellow sweater. Tuesday she wore a tan skirt and a red sweater. Wednesday she wore a white blouse with lace at the collar and a black-and-white checked skirt. Thursday she wore a green skirt and a yellow blouse. Friday she wore a tan suit and a brown blouse. Oh God. Her thighs.

He finished the wine and laid the bottle down carefully on the grass, then lay supine. Her face was above his, the light glinting in her brown eyes. He said her name. He said it again. Bring me this girl, God, he said. I'll do anything, God. He squirmed in his wretchedness.

To eat breakfast in the morning with his mother and sister watching him. Eat, Kenny, Eat, Kenny. What's the matter, Kenny? How could he live through the day? He wanted to die. He would surely die.

Her brown eyes. She loved him. She secretly loved him. She was in bed right now thinking of him, dying of love for him. She was sick of love for him. Monday he would tell her. Or ask her. Monday he would touch her. O dear God, I'm gonna go crazy, he said. I'm gonna die, God. Please. He wanted to masturbate but he couldn't do it with her in his mind, and he didn't want anybody clse.

He looked toward the entrance of the park to see if maybe she was coming to him. In the night.

1950

JACK THE PRIEST
Dark Dark Eros

THE CHIPPED FIGURES of the Holy Family and guests, in their garish colors, one black man with that benevolent face one sees on lawn jockeys. A box in his hands, yellow, adoring, adoring the spastic Saviour. All of them, vulgar in the shabby crèche. Seen through his drunkenness. Further down, the park, the weary Xmas tree he had seen each year since he was born, hung patiently with the desperately ugly cardboard decorations, the lights glimmering. Ah, unhappy, unhappy.

To be fat, nineteen, a fat virgin. Not to have ever touched a breast even beneath bra and sweater. A fat nineteen, a priest. Malaise. Nobody cared for Jack the Priest. He blinked into the warm, unseasonable wind, approaching the park. A rabid masturbator, racked with the moribund Roman Catholic conscience that drove him to Confession whenever he felt his soul unbearably tarnished. The Eucharist, then back to his sexual swamp, desire and tears and desire. Masturbation. Confession. The Pope would sustain him from that thin air of Rome, blessing the soul of him with those two dehydrated, elegant fingers. No hope at home. Xmas. O my God, that tree! That fucking tree. It was actually warmer in the park, the wind straight off the bay with smell of salt and fish, temperate and damp. He walked down the path into the darkness, away from the tree, the air softly radiant from its forty feet of lights. He sat on the grass, then leaned back on his elbows to watch a pale, flabby man walk slowly up the slope toward him. He was a perfection of unattractiveness, simply hopeless. He looked at Jack and sat down next to him.

After some sort of conversation, the man offered Jack a pint of gin and he drank and passed the bottle back. Dixie Belle. The man drank and was then stroking Jack, his hand gentle on the fat thighs. He played with his stiffening penis, then opened his fly and pulled it out. He didn't know how to do it. Jack lay back, giving himself up to whatever pleasure there might be: it was another's hand. The fag was shaking and breathing rapidly, nervous in his good fortune, jerking erratically and crudely, fingering himself too, Jack thought. He came slowly to orgasm, and that, too, was slow, the gradual parting of a wire. The fag left, wiping his hand on his pants.

Jack lay a long time, getting sober, then got up and faced toward the tree. He was chilled through. He had a number of feelings to embrace. To choose. To feel remorse? He felt nothing. Blank. Disgust? Nothing. He was empty, simply uncaring. He imagined the sight of himself, his fat ass, his heavy legs toiling up the path toward the tree. Ah God.

Introduction to sex, he said. Love, he said. He thought that if perhaps he could work on that small glow of self-pity he'd uncovered he might cry. He tried, wrinkling his eyes and distorting his face. He wrenched a sob, and then another, trying to work into some simple expression of feeling. I don't give a shit, he said. He stood at the entrance to the park, looking at the tree, the bulbs and cardboard ornaments heaving in the gusts, colder now. O God! he said. O my God! He tried wrinkling his eyes again and was arrested by the way the lights on the tree smeared, horizontally, in his vision.

1950

CARMINOOTCH
Lester Leaps In

WITH HIS MOTHER AND FATHER away for the weekend, he
asked Ann up on Saturday night. It was almost a magic
for him. There was an immediate feeling that they
would be married here, in this house, the only home he
had ever known, the four old rooms in the walk-up. She
didn't want to come at first, although she loved him.
They were in love, utterly. But he wanted her, she knew
his parents were away, they knew nothing of her, Carmine himself hadn't known exactly how it happened,
but this small, dark girl was suddenly all his life.

She came, at eight, and he made their supper, a kind
of simple elegance given it by the candles he set on the
table, though the meal was hamburger steak and
canned vegetables. He bought a bottle of dollar Bor-
deaux, and used his mother's holiday glasses. After that,
they went into his room and went to bed, simply, it was
precisely clear what they were doing. No persuasion, no
talk of it. Ann was with him until eleven, then she
dressed and left, he would see her tomorrow, they would
walk and take a ride on the ferry, eat clams in Ombrielli's.

When she left, the silence of the familiar apartment
was filled with the sound of his own breath, in his ears.
He touched the sheets, damp and sticky with their fucking, in a kind of awe. He sat, carefully, the chairs were
new to him, he filled this house, a presence of him! His
house, his room, it had never been so much his room.

It was getting late, it had to be after one, there were some sounds of parties from apartments further down the block, and an occasional drunken roar from the Lion's Den at the corner, but the street was, in the main, asleep. The few sounds made it quieter, somehow, to him, he would wake them up, they were all around him, ground into their dead lives, trying to kill him too. He got the tenor out, and put the sling around his neck, then adjusted the reed, and put out all the lights.

He began to blow, softly, keeping the horn full of air, a breathy sound, he had an excellent embouchure, noodling, blowing snatches of Prez tunes, very quiet on the few things he hardly dared blow, "Louisiana" "I Guess I'll Have to Change My Plans," hearing Prez in his head. Then he went to the window, and opened it wide, the cool air over him, his house. His horn, you can all go fuck yourselves, you heroes.

He switched after one bar of "D.B. Blues" right into "Meadowland," honking it, dropping Prez's phrasing, the breathiness, blowing hard like Arnett Cobb, right on the time, hearing the old Red song bounce off the buildings across the street, blowing harder, playing the tune straight, the clear march melody, Ann was his, fuck all you dead bastards, you fuckin patriots! stopping suddenly, smiling in the dark as he heard the first windows open and the enraged, familiar voices of his neighbors.

LEO FINK
Lieutenant, Field Art'y

HE WAS going on and on about it. Nursing his drink, letting the ice slide in and out of his mouth, easing it back into the whiskey and water, comfortable at the bar. Gibby and Carminootch sat and listened, half-listened, Fink went on. A lieutenant in the National Guard, the Fighting Irish, or the Battling Wops, or some damn regiment or other made up of local sons of local sons, returned home from previous maimings and destruction. They wouldn't get *him* in the Army! was number one. Not that he was afraid to go in another war, fight for his country (a *damn* good country, brother!) but this way if he went he'd go with his Outfit. Trained. Esprit de corps. Knowing. Accepted. And an officer. And.

He went on, and away, his blue eyes looking through the murk of the barroom toward the crest of some hill in New York State somewhere, some blasted Army-owned peak of the Catskills, somewhere. He saw flashes there, on the ridge, rounds being dropped in by the battery. *His* battery. *My* battery. Lt. Fink. Lt. Fink, Leo, of the Crusading Immigrants. To save America. To save the Neighborhood, from somebody, for himself and all Loved Ones.

The shells cost $408.23 apiece. Or $304.82. Or $830.42. You shoulda seen them go, them guns. Those guns, he said, being a lieutenant.

Trained, ready for anything with the Boys in the battery. God, wotta terrific buncha guys. Fire, Lt. Fink would say and marvel at the ease with which the government allowed him to spend anybody's money. Soon, rockets! Oboy!

Esprit, he said. (Actually said that.) A *good* buncha kids, the best. God, go anywhere with that outfit. And the caissons go rolling along, Carminootch said. Not far wrong *there,* Carmine, the lieutenant said. He sucked on his ice, gazing at the ridge under bombardment. Fire! Four hundred American bucks. B-U-X, bucks.

1939

CHARLIE TAYLOR
Dark Dark Eros

SUDDENLY, the comic strips opened to him the possibility of the whole erotic world. Black lusts, twisted into whatever channels he could blast out in his mind, gouge out. Those color girls, fashionable, falling down on their lawns, leaping from cars, their skirts flying. Dixie Dugan, Boots and her Buddies, the sweet breasts of blond Toots. And Jane Arden, the girl reporter, at the bottom of the page, she, herself, in color, in her bra and panties, surrounded by clothes for little girls to cut out and put on her, lovingly. He put nothing on her, or, in his mind, he put everything on her to take it off then, laughing in his absolute power. He traced the woman on toilet paper and drew in a crude hole for her cunt, shadowed her crotch, scratched in nipples. Her lopsided penciled face bland and smiling, awaiting her tweed walking suit, hands open at her sides in the pose of the Virgin Mary.

Or he was Tim Tyler or his curly-haired buddy, deep in the jungle, rescuing lovely girls from mad fiends and slave-traders. These blondes would be in his bed at night, he was so kind to them, press close to them, demented in the feeling that buzzed in his hairless groin. Press close to them, almost in tears at his desire, shielding them from the night sounds and terrors of the black forest. Young Tyler, he felt the very pull and stretch of that cartoon skin, felt the body of his invented damsel, was in it. This occurred when he was kind and benevolent.

Most of the time he felt himself in impotent Sadean rage, Jane Arden in his clutches, in a soundproof room in some apartment by the waterfront, holding her at gunpoint on a toilet seat while he waited for her to shit. What seems to be the trouble, my dear—he went into the exact rhetoric of the strips, flushed, deep in his fantasies, the covers over his head, sounds of his mother and father awake in the next room. What seems to be the trouble? And then she would oblige him, blushing deeply and averting her eyes in her shame and embarrassment as she relieved herself. The most depraved nights were those of his dreams of absolute decadence, when he forced Jane to relieve herself fully clothed, watched her greedily as she twisted and squirmed in discomfort, her skirt stained and polluted by her wastes. Ah God! So beautiful! His boyish penis thrilled in its slight erection.

Sometimes Tim Tyler would break in on Charlie's Sadean ogre and rescue the young reporter or Dixie Dugan and think her through a period of bathing and washing her underwear and clothes—then she would find her safe place with him underneath the violet skies of nighttime Africa. Held close in his arms, protected from all monsters, clean and perfumed and utterly grateful. As Tim, he was ashamed at what he had seen in the monster's retreat. Poor Jane. Poor Dixie. But they knew he knew. Clear power.

One day he had an orgasm shinnying up the lamppost and hung there, thinking he would die from the pleasure that passed over him in waves. For weeks he was afraid to climb another lamppost or the trees in the park; the sensation was too intense, too sweet to be allowable. He dreamed again of black Africa, his rifle, his rescued darlings, blond and sweet. Of locked bathrooms in the most remote fastness of wilderness, filled with the protesting grunts of lovely women at stool. Then he suddenly began to masturbate, absolutely naturally, Harold Teen's Lillums before him in nothing but her step-ins. All of them came into his bed, he summoned them by the dozens, his playmates, cartoon women, teachers, girls on the street, all of them waiting in line for the privilege of being transformed into his mattress and sheets, his pillow, his hand. He sweated with delight and fear of retribution, pumping his bed in a frenzy of gratification.

1936

BIG KID
Charlie Taylor

CHARLIE WAS VERY TALL for nine. That, and he had a father, a real father, permanent man, living with him and his mother and sister, Patsy. They were surely ringers, coming from some outlandish city in the South, Richmond or Tuscaloosa, to Brooklyn, the father landing a series of jobs which kept them eating. To say: Charlie's father. Patsy's father. Or Mister Taylor, as he walked home from the subway past the games flowing about him. A desire fell on all of them, fatherless children. The mothers, alone, locked into their stooptalk and endless preparations of vegetable soup, navy beans and salt pork, the cheapest tuna, observed the family with dull longing, or felt, sharply, the memory of a sweet stiff cock up them. A regular cock. A legitimate, husbandly cock. In long nights on the daybed in the living room with the children asleep next door, crowded, in clutter of junk and old clothes, hands on their cunts. The contented Taylor Family.

Charlie Taylor, who gave of his day-old mince cakes from Drewes.

Charlie Taylor, who was afraid of the Dick Tracy serials with the collapsing Brooklyn Bridge, the club-footed shuffle of the Spider.

Charlie Taylor, who wore a gray tweed cabdriver's cap.

Charlie Taylor, who gave everybody whooping cough.

Charlie Taylor, whose socks did not meet, ever, his knickers.

Charlie Taylor, whose father took him to see the Dodgers.

Charlie Taylor, who went to Nathan's once a month for hot dogs and french fries.

A kind boy. With a father and mother. And blond, stupid sister. Whom all the boys adored.

Charlie Taylor, who would not sneak in to the Loew's Alpine.

Charlie Taylor, who thought the Cockroach and all policemen his friends, as he was taught in school.

Charlie Taylor, who blushed for his sister when Artie Salvo gave her a penny ring on whose brass was set under celluloid a color picture of the Virgin Mary. Blushed in deference to this intimacy.

Charlie Taylor, who maintained that only bad women fucked, and that they did it with their belly buttons.

Charlie Taylor, headed for the steady job of reinsurance clerk, where he would carve CT into the yellow enamel of his Mongol pencils.

Whose mother would die of leukemia; whose sister would marry a fireman with acne; whose father would finish as a drunken machinist in Flint.

A tall boy, clear face, gray eyes, slow and friendly.

1938

LITTLE MICKEY

HE WAS the best jumper, although his ribs stuck out. He was the best runner, though he wore no socks. Sneakers falling apart, shreds of canvas and rubber, with the little toes protruding. A face like a mouse, black hair and black eyes. His teeth were bad. His mother sat in Flynn's all night drinking Green River with beer chasers. His shirts were threadbare. He was a fantastic speller. Pray God for him.

Big Mickey was somehow a "cousin" of his, and wished to protect him. Little Mickey resented this, an innate nicety of culture. He fought against Colonel Stinky and his army with great verve and joy, running them in circles. He didn't know how to play ball, it was all too much for him, too much an extension of that nervous body. He ate one meal a day and whatever he could steal in candy from Arnold's. A fine-drawn child.

He was tough and full of tales and bullshit hyperbole. He made up ghost stories to tell at night. He could build a fire in the lot in the strongest wind. He knew where to get the firm clods of earth in the park for dirt bombs. His mother left one night with an elevator operator and never came back. Dear Mickey.

He was kind to Jo-Jo, the idiot, but offhandedly and

casually. He could get from one end of 68th Street to the other through the back yards. He climbed as well as a cat. He stood under the streetlamp smoking. He was not afraid of Black Tom but pretended to be, so as not to spoil the thrills. He was noble.

An aunt took him. He moved a few blocks away but came to the block every day to play. Big Mickey cut his hair and took him crabbing. He sledded down Dead Man's Hill with an elegant daring. He was hungry from morning till night. He never lost at 21 or Knuckles. He had style.

He could roast mickeys so that the meat of the potatoes never dried out. He made up beautiful stories about his father. He could recognize any car, make and date. He hitched on trolley cars blowing great pink bubbles. He ate margarine and brown sugar on stale bread. Selah.

His aunt took him away to Pittsburgh. He wrote a letter to everybody, in care of Big Mickey. It was sober and well-composed, and full of news. Big Mickey read it to all the boys one night under a light in the park. They sat carefully, feeling masculine and mature. This letter to them, this really important event. In it Mickey said, "You are the best guys I ever knew in my life." His voice was crystal through the penciled words on the loose-leaf paper. Dear, dear Mickey.

1949

---

* GIRLS * GIRLS * GIRLS *
Jack the Priest

STORIES, all lies, or mostly lies, coming in at him. Flown in, coasted in, straight into that ear, propped against the fat head, rolls of flesh, the feathery beard. All the broads, what they did, what could be done to them, oo-eee! they all like it, babes, up the ole gash, slip it in, bang it up, they can't fool guys like me. The stories went on, a mass effort to torture Jack the Fat. Jackie the Priest, who's got himself that good ole girlfriend, Mary Fist. OK? You get it, Carminootch? Gibby babes? Mary Fist. A-ho. A-ha. Jack didn't care, lies or not, he listened, every day, every chance he got. He could figure anyway, it was possible that it could happen, right? Girls were . . . they just were only . . . *people,* right? They DID want it. Up the box.

Legs, tits, titties, boobs, assholes, cunts, black stockings, panties, girdles, corsets, garter belts, bras, lace and silk and nylon, and ankles, mouths, teeth, the box, the cunt, the gash, the twat, the hole, the snatch, the split, the slit, the pussy, the slot, everything. Before his eyes. Now Carminootch would lie, then Gibby, then Donnie G. Pete, Glade, even Sprenger. There was that fanatic need in his eyes, not that he'd never got laid, but that he never would. It couldn't be possible, Jack would think, in tears, in bed, playing with himself. Grow up to be a moron. God, they hit on him without mercy.

He didn't believe all of it, but it didn't matter. The words tore at and ravaged him. The story that had him in a daze of restless lust for a week, from Joe Kane about the Catholic broad (There was the old one, also by Joe, about the broad met him at the door with no clothes on, led him upstairs with her parents away for the weekend, and blew him in the shower. Wow! Oh, Jesus.): the good Catholic broad, Irish Catholic, Jackie kid, nothin ever touched her below the waist but a warm washcloth. I give this hot book with photographs, from Paris, to her in school, just smilin at her. A real black-haired beauty, belongs to the Sodality of the Sacred Heart, right? Alla same, babe. Then one day later, Joe goes to get his book, he's feelin a little ashamed, right Jackie? Hey, Cheech, I tole you this story, right? Cheech is smiling and moving his hips, they're leaning on the lamppost on the corner. I get there, she lets me in, nobody's home, her old man and mother hadda go somewhere, she's inna nightgown, come in an have a cold drink, hey, it's hot that night. I go in ta take a piss, I come out, she's bare-ass naked, with the book in her hand, sittin on the couch. Hey? I wanna do everything that's in this book, Joe, she says. *Everything.* Jack is struck dumb at the thought of this virgin Irish Catholic girl, he thinks of her in Confession, oh God! The priest behind his grille flushed in the darkness.

Not to be able to look at a woman on the streets for a week, or maybe more. That black hair: to hear that voice: Jack, darling (breathy), everything. Every Thing.

IN THE PARK
The Stroller

FAT GEORGE walked under the trees toward the Third Avenue tunnel. He was smoking, looking up at the stars occasionally, blue and alone. The repetitive clamor of Yodel's had got to him this evening and he had started home early, but then had moved toward the park to walk down to the pier, maybe have some clams at Ombrielli's, back in the beer garden, alone. A pitcher of beer, maybe two, they never asked his age there. He stopped under a tree and sat down on the grass, the salt breeze from the bay crossing over him, the young leaves moving quietly, a whisper at the tops of the old trees. He lay back then and lit another cigarette. Someone should have something to say to him, a girl? Some girl could really like him? Why not. Fink, the bastard, with that whore Pat whatsername, her box shoved out in front of her like there was something wrong with her, like a cripple, her ass shoved up on top of her hips.

Pat, he thought. Fink. Pat. He rubbed his crotch. Oh, Jesus. Walking again, under the tunnel, then up the path across the road that cut through to the Belt Parkway. He saw a movement under some trees and stopped, sidestepped into dense shadow and moved along the path quietly, embarrassed. Lovers, necking, they were in front of him then alongside as he moved, his head forward, eyes jammed over to them. Johnny Dobbs and Cooky, her blouse was open, Johnny's head was down between her breasts, his whole arm lost under her skirt. She was groping at his fly.

I doan need that, George said, fuck that. The pinhead
bastard and Cooky! Cooky! Ya gotta be crazy. Cooky . . .
He crossed the roadway again and climbed the steep
grassy hill on the other side, up to the fence bordering
the street, the knoll of the ridge grown close with crab
apple trees. Then he worked his way back along the
knoll, crouching and duckwalking, keeping behind the
trees as much as possible, till he was directly opposite
them. He settled himself between the trunks of two
trees and peered across at the two bodies but they were
flat on the grass now, he caught glints of light from
Johnny's white shirt. Nothing to be seen. He peered,
straining his eyes, neck craned forward, but there was
still only the occasional flashes of white. But they were
fucking, no doubt of that, they were fucking, the numb-
skull bastard and his cunt! Fat George opened his fly and
began to masturbate, his eyes tearing, the white flashes
hazed and blurry, Fink and Pat, you bastards, probly at
a fuckin *dance* tonight! He swiped his free hand viciously against the bark of the tree.

1948

THE RAPE
Penny

PENNY WAS TALL AND PALE. Her clothes were unfashion-
able, and fit her badly. She wore rimless glasses, and her
hair in tight unnatural curls. Her legs were sticklike,
but her breasts were heavy and youthful. She was about
twenty-five, the organist for the White Robed Choir in
the holy coalbox Baptist church across from Yodel's. She
had a dazed look. After choir practice, on Tuesday and
Thursday nights, she came into Yodel's for a half pint of

vanilla ice cream and the *News*. It was inalterable, although once in a while she would also buy a *Silver Screen*.

One night, she came in with her white robe on, it was mild and summery and she hadn't bothered to change. Her clothes were in a brown paper bag under her arm. She squinted at Phil and ordered her ice cream, staring at the headline of the *News* for a long time, tapping a half-dollar on the marble counter. A beautiful robe! A truly bee-yoo-teeful robe, Al said. His hat was in his hand, the light glittering on his glasses and gold tooth. Penny gazed at him and her mouth opened a little, those tiny lips, thin and scarlet. Oh, she said. She didn't remember ever seeing Al before. Are you with—the—congregation? he said. Oh, she said, again. She was looking at his gold tooth, the light off it. Phil gave her the ice cream and she paid him. Oh, yes, I play the organ—for the choir.

Too good to be true. Al was looking at her breasts, thinking of them bare, heavy, a little upturn at the tips with the tight brown nipples. I'm so delighted! he said. Delighted! I play myself, drummer. A crackerjack too, right, Philip! You got it, Al baby, Phil said. He was scratching his crotch, reading the sports page. Terrific! I'd be delighted to hear you play, Al said. However, I'm afraid that I'm not of—I should say, I am not a—religious man. Penny felt the cold of the ice cream through her robe and slip, a delicate subtle touch on her flesh. Oh! Oh, that's all right, come over on Friday night, everybody is welcome to the church. Pastor Johnson is delighted to meet new people, anytime. Oh, please come. You'll be *so* welcome. Her flesh was tingling now, she could feel a secret warmth in her belly, down between her legs a delicious irritation. Al's glasses shimmered. I might be too much of a sinner, Al said. He was working the fucking clothes right the fuck off her, over

44

the hips, over the head, oh baby! She laughed, stiff. Oh, no one is turned away by Pastor Johnson. Well, if I could be sure that you'd be there, Miss—? My name is Penny Caade. Oh yes, I'll be there. Do come, it will be such a warm experience, and we'd be honored to have a musician there. My honor, Miss Caade, all honor to an organist.

They talked another moment and he watched her leave. He put his hat back on, he took his hat off, he put his hat back on. Philip! he said. Did you see those mammaries, Philip! Kee-rist! Ah shit, Al. That's Penny. *Penny.*

Nickel, dime, or quarter, Philip, no one, and you can bet your sweet little ass, not Uncle Al, can pass up those supREME titties! I shall join in the songs of my childhood next Friday night. The old ragged cross. The cock of ages! Ahaha*ha,* Philip, the cock of ages, a juddy, no? A juddy, Philip, a juddy, no, cock of ages, juddy, Philip? Philip?

1948

THE RAPE
The Rape

THE GAME WAS GOING ON, it was going on and getting deeper, serious, and Penny had absolutely no idea how to stop it. In her apartment! Al, sitting in the easy chair now, flipping through a magazine, after a flurry of pinches and kisses and caresses. She was flustered and perspiring. Excited, but unable to handle it. To actually be here, with this man, Al. He was a good man. But his attentions had been real, far different from the goodnight kisses of the past month. She had noticed a cooling in him, he had missed a number of meetings in the church.

(Playing the organ, her eye on the door. No one entering, the walk home with her ice cream and paper.)

But he was so warm at being invited to dinner. He shone, his face was pink. And his glittering tooth stabbed its light at her, that wide grin, his hat swept off. Each movement memorized. Thinking of the hardness of his—member—against her thigh. She brushed against him once, the back of her hand, consciously, it burned, it burned her. She felt the cylindrical firmness on her hand until she had fallen asleep.

He *wanted* to come to dinner. Now he looked through a magazine. She was cooking, almost all ready, he would like her ragout.

The knowledge that it was drying out in the pot, ruined. He was over her on the couch, his glasses on the end table, the fragility of them, the gold frames so slender, the fine-ground lenses, brilliant in the lamplight. His watering eyes, burning. His tongue between his teeth. She knew her skirt was up to her hips, her thighs half-spread, she exposed to him. Lying as drugged, terrified and waiting. He would not really. He could wait. They would honeymoon, to Miami, Palm Beach, Silver Springs. His groin thrust forward, his hands moving at his buckle. Where you could see the fishes and coral and plants through the glass bottoms of boats.

His eyes, burning and watering. He was licking her whole face as he grunted and rammed into her. She felt such exquisite pleasure, the enormous *size* of it. The pain was dull, simple. She reached down and cupped his heavy balls in her hand and felt the stickiness, the wet. Oh, she groaned, and moved toward him, shoved her hips forward to meet his thrust. The smell of burning from the kitchen as the meat stuck, smoldering, to the bottom of the pot.

There was so much blood. He was disgusted, and surprised. He said a few things, washing in the bathroom. She lay down gingerly, in a terrycloth robe, the ragout off the stove and the window open. We can have a salad! she said gaily, beginning to cry. She looked at the couch, stained deep, soaking wet in spots. She pushed the robe between her legs.

Was he actually tearing at her finger?

Without anger, simple determination.

He wanted the ring. She had wrapped adhesive tape around the band so that it would fit her finger. He was having a great deal of trouble. He got it off and left. She stood looking at the bloody couch, the acrid smell of scorched food pervading the room.

1940

SEXOLOGY: 100 FACTS

1. IF YOU jerk off you get hairy palms.
2. If you jerk off you go crazy.
3. If you jerk off you go to hell.
4. If you jerk off you can't fuck when you get married.
5. If you jerk off you won't like girls.
6. If you jerk off you get a heart attack.
7. If you jerk off you get a stroke.
8. If you jerk off you get pimples.
9. If you jerk off you get boils.
10. If you jerk off you squint.
11. If you jerk off you go blind.
12. If you jerk off you become a sex fiend.
13. If you jerk off you run out of juice.
14. If you jerk off your balls dry up.
15. If you jerk off you die.
16. Girls fuck themselves with bananas.
17. Girls fuck themselves with frankfurters.

18. Girls fuck themselves with candles.
19. Girls fuck themselves with gearshifts.
20. Girls fuck themselves with their fingers.
21. Girls fuck themselves with soda bottles.
22. Girls can pull their guts out fucking themselves with soda bottles.
23. Jewish girls love to fuck.
24. Clean girls won't suck cock.
25. All girls deep down love to suck cock.
26. Fags are afraid of girls.
27. Girls are afraid of fags.
28. Your mother doesn't really fuck.
29. Your mother fucked a couple of times accidentally.
30. Your father loves your mother too much to fuck her.
31. Nobody's mother ever sucked a cock.
32. Having a baby is dirty.
33. You can't piss in a girl.
34. A girl can't piss with a guy inside her.
35. Your sister will never fuck anybody but her husband when he comes along.
36. If you play with your sister you'll both go crazy.
37. If you play with your sister you'll both go to hell.
38. Priests fuck nuns.
39. Priests fuck each other.
40. Priests suck each other.
41. Nuns fuck each other with dildoes.
42. Nuns suck each other.
43. Girls love to play with each other.
44. Morphodites can fuck themselves.
45. You can get stuck in a girl's asshole.
46. You can get stuck in a girl's cunt and they have to operate on you.
47. You get the clap easiest from toilet seats in the subway.

48. Rubbers always break when you come.
49. Girls are always ready to fuck.
50. Bowlegged girls fuck a lot.
51. Girls with big tits are whores.
52. A girl's mouth is the same size as her cunt.
53. If a girl's nipples get hard, she's hot.
54. If a girl French-kisses you, you can fuck her.
55. Girls like to make you come in your pants.
56. Dirty books and pictures make you a moron.
57. Girls with pimples are whores.
58. Girls with pimples have the clap.
59. The clap is syphilis.
60. Syphilis can't be cured except once in a while by praying.
61. If you get the clap your cock falls off in a few years.
62. Girls hardly ever get the clap.
63. If girls get the clap it doesn't bother them.
64. If you eat pussy you're a maniac.
65. If you eat pussy you're a moron.
66. If you eat pussy you'll become a sex fiend.
67. If you eat pussy you'll do anything.
68. Only guys who can't fuck eat pussy.
69. All Hollywood actors are really fags.
70. All artists are fags.
71. All Frenchmen like to eat pussy.
72. All Italians are good fuckers.
73. All niggers have gigantic cocks.
74. Niggers can split white girls in two with their cocks.
75. There are no nigger fags.
76. Shepherds all fuck sheep.
77. Sheep love to be fucked by humans.
78. All girls can take a horse cock in them.
79. Greeks like to fuck girls in the ass.
80. Greeks like to fuck guys in the ass.

81. If you fuck a girl in the ass once, she won't let you fuck her any other way.
82. You get piles from getting fucked in the ass.
83. If you have piles it means you got fucked in the ass once.
84. You can circumcise yourself fucking a virgin.
85. There are some good-looking teachers who make their pupils fuck them.
86. There's a girl in Bensonhurst who barks when you fuck her.
87. There's a girl in Marine Park who says prayers when you fuck her.
88. Reefers make you a sex fiend.
89. If you meet a girl who lets you take her under the Coney Island boardwalk she'll suck you off.
90. Gypsy fortune-tellers at Coney Island are really whores.
91. There was a guy from Ovington Avenue who came in his summer pants at the church dance with his date.
92. Spanish fly makes any girl go crazy for a fuck.
93. Spanish fly has no effect on men.
94. A girl in Flatbush fucked everybody on her block after she took a Spanish fly pill.
95. You can get Spanish fly on Union Street.
96. If somebody comes in your eyes you go stone blind.
97. Real whores love to swallow come.
98. Virgins are the best fucks.
99. Men have to teach girls how to fuck.
100. Girls shoot a load like men when they come.

GIBBY
From a Diary

24 MAY 1950

Ruth . . . Ruth . . . Ruth . . . I can think of only her lately
—God! But she is in my bloodstream . . . she is part
of me—her touch warm, thrilling—her eyes, the sea,
gray-green, making me dizzy. I can see no one else—I
compare all other women to her lithe, sweet body—oh
God, but she is lovely in form and mind—she is lovely,
lovely, lovely—Eyes of the sea—I'll never forget her
eyes—you look into them and are lost—they are fathom-
less, bottomless as the sea. On the 9th of March in this
book I wrote that I wanted only her body—that I was
reading loveliness into a possible relationship above the
mere physical act—in other words (why in the name of
Christ don't I come out with it! Coward!) love. But now,
oh, now now now—thick lump in my chest at the
thought of her—sweet desire in my throat at the thought
of her—all of me wanting her, scheming to see her, talk
to her—like a goddamned high-school boy with his first
crush. Eyes driving me mad—and I—I afraid to tell her
—afraid to make a fool of myself—and soon the Army
will beckon—the Army becomes my life—and still
afraid to say anything—still just hinting, scheming,
mad to see her—God! God! But she is a wholeness in
chaos, she is always, always, an elemental, within me—
endless as the sea—her eyes are she—beautiful as the
sea—Ruth of sea-eyes, Ruth, I am falling in love with
you.

27 May 1950

O Ruth! I said it not but you knew—you knew O my darling Ruth—Never has a night been lovelier than that, sweet Ruth of sea-eyes. And these two days have been endless—I long for you—I wait for you. I wait to see you tomorrow my Ruth—my darling Ruth—Oh but I grow dizzy with the thought of you—your kisses and firm body—your lovely eyes deep in mine, mouth on mine my Ruth, my Ruth of sea-eyes—and I have found you—I have found you and I feel myself deeply in your heart—loved by you; loved by you, Ruth—I am loved—O God! O Christ! But can a man love you as much as I can? —can I love you as much as I want to? I spin when I think of you—your tenderness that night—O Ruth! One month I have with you before you must leave for a time —one month that I must make a thousand years—I must freeze the month—stop the shuttling time, slow it, damn it! Ruth, one month and I love you Ruth, I love you—we will live, live, live and love and damn the world; Oh, the down on your upper lip is beaten gold, your breasts are more beautiful than clouds in spring—O Ruth you will never die in me—until I die—you are my love, Ruth, my love, my Ruth of sea-eyes.

1935

BACON & EGGS

Fake bitter dignity of the poor
underneath which
desperation. thrives and writhes
                GIBBY and his mother would be
presented at various times with different foully given

necessities by his grandmother: construed by her as Gifts. One of these, the most regularly offered, each Sunday, was two eggs and two strips of bacon, carefully laid in a small brown paper bag, which Gibby and his mother went to get at ten o'clock after mass. The righteousness of the giving. Gibby would feel sick, a sinking or weightlessness of his crotch; his mother's face still and composed. The dear, desperate wish for his grandmother's death crawled through him. Oh, it was a monster to be welcomed, in fear and guilt.

One Sunday, climbing their stoop, the bag in his mother's hand, Gibby tripped and his mother reached out to grab him, so that the bag fell. The eggs were smashed and the bacon gummy with their insides. In the house was oatmeal. Nourishing.

They walked around the corner again to the grandmother's apartment, his mother holding the soggy bag, the evidence. In that fake, numb dignity. She *was* her mother, and his grandmother. Though gnawed and decayed by greed, a sliver? of care?

But there was no new gift of eggs, instead a harangue about her carelessness, and his carelessness, big-footed and clumsy (his father's blood had poisoned him). You can do without good eggs, she said. Don't deserve em. They cost good money. All of which was good, good, good. It's your grandfather who works for those eggs, *your* father. Maybe next Sunday you'll be more careful and watch that boy, teach him how to walk. Seven years old!

So they stood, stiff against misery and rage, the grandfather in his chair with the *News* rotogravure open in front of him, reading of a man in Decatur who had built a scale model of the Brooklyn Bridge out of toothpicks. Hero, breadwinner, eggbuyer.

1938

SHINING GREEN COUPE

Under his gray stained fedora his blue eyes were evil and hard. He'd get the goddam kid on the car, get one of the little bastards anyway!

The kid was Artie Salvo, small and dark, maybe eight or nine years old, his threadbare and faded corduroys rubbing against the fender of the dark green Plymouth coupe he sat on. Shined! Washed and washed again! And rinsed! And laboriously Simonized to a dull luster, rich, the sun in highlights off it. And this greaser kid on it.

This hero, fair of hair, blue of eye, jumped out from the doorway and grabbed Artie as he was jumping off the fender to Angus' shouted chicky! But it was too late and the car-owner had his arm and was twisting it. Dago son of a bitch, ruin my car? Ruin my car? Ruin my car, hah? Ruin my *car?* Artie was twisting and squirming to get away, cursing as the man whacked him across the ass and legs with his large, hard hand. Then threw him away from him so that Artie stumbled and fell.

It was the car, the very fact of it. In this year of depression to have this vehicle. Symbol of hope and re-generation, a sock full of golden eagles sewn into the mattress. Our hero had bought stock in America. No greasy-haired Dago bastard was going to sully that.

Later the hero was drafted and the block learned he was killed in Italy. Perhaps some distant relative of the Salvo family, jovially laughing in that well-known and beloved Italian manner, full of wine and pasta, pictures of his curly-haired children in his wallet, dreaming of

54

peace and his little fig grove, had put a Fascisti bullet through his head, relieving him forever of his American dream.

1940

THE STREAMLINER

Looka that! Bubbsy said. They were playing in the weeds next to the hurricane fence that bordered the Long Island yards below, and they ran to the fence where Bubbsy was standing, clutching at the wire, looking down into the cut. Fink didn't run though, but came up after them, slowly, licking voluptuously at his vanilla cone. Wow! Duck said, a streamliner! It's a streamliner all right, Donnie said. Looka the tables in that car with the white tablecloths an flowers.

Fink was there now, and looked down with them, detached, intent on his ice cream. You still got that goddam ice cream cone? Duck said. The damn thing'll melt on ya. Fink looked at him, eyes half-closed. You guys eat too fast an then you just wonder why I got mine left. Mmm. This is *good* ice cream. Tastes better when you eat it slow. They watched him lick the ice cream, working the scoop into a point. I hope the goddam thing melts all over ya, Duck said. Ah looka the train! Bubbsy said. It's switchin tracks. God, what a beauty! Woddaya thinka that, Finky? You ever see anything like that? Donnie said.

Fink looked down at it, still working gingerly at the cone. Looks kinda tinny, he said. They looked at him, then back at the streamliner. None of them had ever seen a streamliner before, and they looked back at Fink. He was delicately nibbling at the rim of the cone itself, they could hear the slight crackling it made as he worked his way around full circle. I can't help it, he said, I just think it looks kinda tinny. Cheap lookin. Maybe it's the colors, green an yellow, maybe that's it. It looks kinda like a kid's toy—a little kid's. Like a nalectric train.

Some of the boys looked at him, and some at the train, moving slowly now past a string of boxcars at the far side of the yards. Donnie picked up a stone and fired it up in the air, over the fence in a high parabola, watched it come down and bounce on the slope beyond, roll a few feet and stop. Oh shit, he said. Oh for God sake, Fink.

1937

BEER

IN THE HOT SUMMER NIGHTS, on the stoops, through ground-floor windows passed gingerly, with tenderest care, pitchers, glasses, cans and containers of every shape, pots. On corners, in the park, under trees, in doorways. Sweating glasses, icy, tart-cold, the fresh cream head, down the throats of the hopeless men, the deserted women, the boys who would be dead and maimed in five more years, the children with a sip or two. Balm, ointment, air-conditioning. Nectar and love and friendship together. To dull the view of despair, to tranquilize, to lift the spirits, to aid sleep, to wash down the hash and home fries, the macaroni and cheese, the spaghetti with oleo, the stale bread.

To make disappear the cockroaches and mice. To be cat, dog, bird, monkey, svelte tiger in the zoo, silent goldfish and turtle. To be lover, mistress, vivacious pornographic blondes. To be Clark Gable and Fred Astaire and William Powell. To be Carole Lombard, Madeleine Carroll, Irene Dunne. To assist the dream. To be dream.

To make the street the mountains, the beaches, the clear swift creek. To bring to the corner Jack Benny and Fred Allen. To be Mr. First-Nighter and Mr. District Attorney. To stagger into the universe of Jack, Doc, and Reggie. To love a mystery. To use Lux in sweet abandon. To make the teeth brilliant with Ipana. To make the father return to that street, smiling, with money. With a new hat.

To be loved, and again loved, to be wanted. To have a job. To break the teeth of the home-relief investigator. To crush the waxy orange cheese under foot. To get out.

Hot summer, borne more easily with it, a hope in it, cold, wet, the cans of it, the lid floating on the bubbling head. Buckets of it, buckets of suds. Relief.

1938

THE MAGNIFICENT MUSIC MACHINE

FLYNN'S JUKEBOX. The customer dropped in a nickel or a dime or a quarter and a voice answered him, a real voice, a girl's voice, quiet and pleasant. Warm. She asked him what selections he wanted and he answered. Then they were played. It was a fantasy. It was brilliant. Some sort of telephone arrangement, or something similar. She was a real girl and she listened to the men ask. Talked to them.

Some of them went half-mad talking to her, they played the same tune over and over all night. Some of them hugged the jukebox and cried, kicked it, propositioned it. Let's fuck, sister! Come on outa that fuckin jukebox and let's fuck! The pride of the neighborhood.

They cursed and sobbed: sober, they carried on flirtatious conversations. The women hated her.

The kids stood outside the back door in the evenings amazed, staring. The great, shining machine, all lights and the girl's voice. There were hundreds of selections. She talked. Once in a while she laughed. Some of the men fell in love with her and went home and wouldn't speak to their wives, or fucked them, their heads full of the girl's voice. The kids thought she was in the machine, so did some of the men. Come out! Come outa there, you bitch! And Flynn would throw them out and point them home.

Some thought she was in the cellar in some special soundproof room, surrounded by gadgets and records and microphones. Hell, they'd all seen radio stations in the movies. She sat, just beneath their beer-heavy feet. Maybe she was. Maybe she really was. Some lustrous-haired virgin. In dreams I kiss your hand, madame.

1951

68th STREET
2 A.M.

IT HAD BEEN a bad night in every way. Gibby had wanted simply to get drunk alone, out of the neighborhood, so that he wouldn't run into anyone he knew. Some vestige of Hollywoodiana left in him dictated this. But he started in the Melody Room, hoping he'd meet someone —later, he could go away, alone, take a cab, to Flatbush, to be near her, anyway, near her house, perhaps he would even see her. He had rehearsed in his head his look, the whole expression, the words would come in a pattern of exhausted bitterness.

He met Carmine, already half-shot, alone at the far end of the bar, reddish in the glow from the jukebox. Heart of my heart. How I love that melody, it said, a fake barbershop quartet. Ann had left him, to marry some fruit-store owner, a Greek. Selected by the family. Her hands will be black and grimy from stroking quarters, Black Mac had said. It was funny to everybody but Carmine. Gibby sat down next to him and ordered a whiskey and ale. As he thought that he wouldn't tell him, at that exact moment, he told him. She didn't love him, didn't want to see him any more, and he was going in the fuckin Army next week! Carmine nodded, and backed up Gibby's drink. They played tunes, the intimations of which were utterly private to each, subtleties of place and time in them, the young Irish drunks filling up the bar with their rep stripe ties and blue straw hats. Wash and wear. Where's Glade? Carmine said. This fuckin place looks like Dublin. In Gallagher's probly, Gibby said. With the Norwegian seamen. They laughed.

Drunk, falling down drunk, and with great bravado, they reeled up Ovington Avenue toward Fourth. To get a hamburger in the Royal. Great bravado. Gibby felt his heart would stop, he was so full of her, and he heard his voice outside himself, through some ear that was still sober, unutterably clear and cold. Carmine was sick now, puking in the gutter, Gibby holding him. He imagined her looking at him, in sympathy, holding up his friend, and he smiled into the darkness where he was placing her. Yellow skirt, a blue print blouse, she was fair. Carmine was crying, Ann, my dear Ann, my dear Ann, he was blubbering through his spit and vomit, swaying in his crouch, and Gibby rubbed his back. Fuck the Army, Gibby said, fuck Korea, he said, fuck Brooklyn, fuck this neighborhood. Ann, Carmine said. It was a kind of whisper, to her, she was across the street, bright and cool, in the shadows with the fair girl, they were hand in hand, the drunks squinted at them.

They were in the Royal but it was jammed. Fink, the Dobbs brothers, Whitey the Greek, Eddy Bromo, Al, Eddy Beshary, the counter was packed, the tables. Fat George came up to them, his car keys in his hand. Less get some white clam, he said. I got the wheels. They said something, too late, or something, they were sad and beaten. Harry the waiter dashed about, Gentlemen, gentlemen, he said, the coffees on his arms, sloshing into the saucers. Maybe Ann's . . . Carmine began, looking for her. No Greek fruit-peddlers there, no Ann, nobody. Everybody, drunk, shouting, the gang, the tired night here, ending, Saturday. A fight or two bubbling in the air, in careless conversation, waiting for somebody to take advantage of something. Shaerbach's kid brother in his uniform, his cunt cap pushed back on his shaved, Neanderthal skull, jump boots scuffed and dulled, selecting a record, "Hello Young Lovers." The cretin basted, Gibby said to Fat George. I'm goin, George said. They walked out with him, the street was absolutely silent and deserted, foggy. George crossed over to his car, ya sure? he said. White clam? we got time ta make it. No, Gibby said. Carmine leaned on him. They walked slowly to Triangle Park, past the new extension on the Cities Service lot, the holy coalbox gone, past the new A & P on the old tennis court, past the new Baptist church, the doorway right where they used to roast mickeys. They sat in the park, and it began to drizzle, they sat, getting sober, thirsty. Let's get some ice coffee ta go from Harry, Gibby said. We can come back and drink it here. It's rainin, Carmine said, that's what we need, right? Fuck the rain, Gibby said.

They walked back. There was something, some hulk, on the mailbox just outside Yodel's. As they got closer,

60

they could see it was somebody sitting there, in the drizzle, his legs crossed, Indian style, his head hanging down
on his chest. Sprenger, Gibby said. Sprenger, he called.
You think you'll grow, there? He's a fuckin plant, a fuckin geranium, Carmine said. Sprenger looked up at them,
his eyes were vacant, the dried spittle around his lips,
crusted. Nobody's around, he said. A fuckin geranium is
right, Gibby said. The three of them looked at the sidewalk, suddenly. Gibby was defeated and lost, absolutely
alone. He was reddening, ashamed, uncertainly
ashamed for everything.

1951

68th STREET
4 A.M.

SPRENGER was more awake now, aware that he was wet
from the rain, which had just about stopped. He was
uncomfortable, but he didn't change his position on the
mailbox, just shifted a little, his buttocks numb, and his
legs cramped. There was nothing. He looked down the
street, the light, yellow from the Royal, flashed out on
the slick pavements. There was nothing. He would sit
here, or he would sit someplace. The park. The pier.
Home. Walk. Sit on a stoop. He wasn't so old, he felt, he
was really young. I'm young, he said. His voice broke
phlegmy in the whisper. He saw Johnny Dobbs and
Lately come out of the Royal and look down toward him,
then start walking slowly his way, a good six feet between them, weaving a little. He knew they'd be mean,
the edge off their booze. They stopped in front of him.

A disgrace ta the neighborhood, Johnny said. Right,
Jimmy said. I think we oughta knock the shit out of im.

You hit him, Jimmy said, let's see ya knock him off with one good shot. Sprenger sat there, looking at them. He thought of saying something, not to protest, but something, some word. If he could get angry, furious, he would, simply, kill them. There was no anger in him. A vast apathy. He felt Dobbs' blow, hard against his jawbone and a quick pain there where the skin was split and he was on the ground, sprawling.

Jimmy pulled clumsily at his collar and tried to haul him up but the shirt ripped and Sprenger went down again, propped now on his elbows. The fuckin prick! Johnny screamed, enraged that Sprenger looked at both of them calmly, his hand automatically rubbing his jaw. Johnny kicked him in the side. Hey John now, Jimmy said, hey John. You don't wanna fuck him up. *You* hit him, *you* hit him, goddammit! Johnny yelled, the creep, the creepy moron basted! Get up, he said, get up, Sprenger, ya fuck! Sprenger got up, holding his side. There was nothing, the park, the stoops, he could, maybe, walk? Walk away? Jimmy hit him under the eye and Sprenger staggered, but stood. Hit im again, Jimmy. Hit the creep again! Looka the fuckin filth on im! Jimmy hit him under the heart, hoping he'd just fall down and roll over, but Sprenger stood there, his eye swollen almost shut. Johnny hit him again once on the jaw, and stepped back, then hit him again with the same hand in the same spot, and Sprenger went down. The creep! Filthy! Jimmy was leading him away, and Johnny spat on Sprenger, lying there, bleeding under his eye and from his chin. He watched them walk toward the park, playfully cuffing at one another. They were friends, he thought. He looked around. Maybe he should wash up in the Royal? It was possible. Why not? Why not just walk down to the Royal, and wash up? Maybe have some coffee. And a Danish? But wash up.

1945

G.D.L.A.M.F.
The Demons

THAT WAS a mostly Irish gang, from downtown, around Sunset Park. But those in positions of authority, the warlord and the leader, were Italian. Gingerillas. From their specific modes of living, walk, talk, and dress, the whole gang took its style. The low-class Italian style of the day was that of the bottom dog—the fact that Puerto Ricans would someday occupy their niche as accepted urban filth never occurred to them, so they literally *remembered* the rats behind the shoemaker shop, into whose two-room apartment they had been born. They were tough. The Irish kids, affiliated by "faith," were tough too.

But this gang was withering. There was no one to go down with. The rumor was that they were a brother gang to the Smitty Boys, a rightly feared mob of head-breakers. So no other gang attacked them—and since they could not attack another gang without subsequently involving the Smitties, they lived in peace.

But they knew of the neighborhood around the "other" park, the candy store where creeps hung out, the heterogeneous crowd including nuts, hoods, ex-cons, and gamblers. It was a tough enough place to raid, but not formally organized: they could fuck the place up without feeling cheap, and at the same time know that they weren't getting into a war.

So one night, about fifteen of them, with the consent of the warlord, who didn't come, moved down Fifth Ave-

nue to 68th and 69th Streets and then down toward
Fourth. Any kid with drapes and a duck's ass haircut on
the street got his lumps right away. They'd split up on
Fourth and go to Yodel's and the poolroom, lay out some
of those yoyos and get back to Sunset quick.

Hollywood Sal was in front of the Royal when he saw
them lumping Angie LaRosa across the street in front of
the diner. He ran up to Sal's to tell everybody. Frank Bull
was there, and the Pavolites brothers, Whitey the Greek,
and some others.

Whitey ran down to Phil's with Hermes and Doc,
getting out of the poolroom just as two Demons came
in and up. The first kid had a hawk face, with acne scars,
and his name, across his left breast in red script, read
"Paddy." Frank hit him in the head with a cueball,
shrieking, Looka this fuckin momo! Looka this fuckin
momo! "Paddy" went down and the guy behind stumbled over him and Dick Tracy hit him over the head
with his stick. On the street, Doc was holding some fat
Neapolitan while Hollywood Sal broke his mouth. In
Yodel's, Phil watched three Demons knocking his Ko-
Kets and Charms on the floor for a moment and then
saw Hermes and Whitey come in with Jimmy Lately
and some hard-looking guy from Coney Island. Jimmy
got kicked in the balls, but the three Demons got thrown
out on the street into a circle of smaller kids, who kicked
and spit at them. The Cockroach went shooting into the
men's room in Pat's, then realized he could run across
Fourth Avenue and down to Fifth to get a patrol car
up.

The Demons were on the way home now, one taking
a whack at Hermes with a weighted broomstick as he
dodged toward the parked cars, and then in and out
between them, running straight for Third Avenue.

When the cops got there, the only people around were
two of the Demons, lumped and bloody. The cops

slapped and pushed them for a minute or two, then told them to get the fuck back where they belonged. They weren't too hard on them because they were both Irish kids. The Cockroach stood behind the other cops, stroking his nightstick and mumbling about tearing their legs the fuck off them.

When the cops got around to checking the Royal, Hollywood Sal was on a second Danish. He looked up from the results and nodded a smile at them from under his black-and-white-checked porkpie.

1951

MONTE THE COUNT
They Won't Hurt You

IN THE CAB he knew where he was going, and it seemed as if he didn't care. But perhaps he didn't know, or thought of it as something else. A checkup: going back in the Army: moving out, again, somewhere, toward the sound of guns. In bright sunlight. There was snow on the ground, that too, and the mud in the parks and under the trees along the streets, here and there. Army mud. It could have been a six-by? But not enough rattling.

Mac was looking at him and having a great deal of trouble doing it, his face so vacant, looking out first one window, then through the windshield, then the other side, then back. The fine scars stood out on his face, the broken nose mushy. Where the plate in his head was the hair grew sparse and wiry.

For only an examination, Monte, Mac said. They keep ya overnight, or a coupla days, bang! ya back with the guys. Monte looked out the window. They gonna put me away good, Mac, they gonna get all them fuckin cops down there an they're gonna talk about me an my head an all that shit.

His head was important. Mac knew that, it was the thing. Maybe his brain got touched a little after all? They won't hurt ya, Monte, they won't hurt ya . . . but they gotta take a look at ya—you been fuckin up a lotta bars. The cabdriver turned his head impatiently. I'm gonna take Eastern Parkway, chief. OK? OK, Mac said. That's OK *chief!* Monte said. Yeah, *chief!* Take it easy, Count, Mac said. He rubbed his knee tenderly.

They're gonna fuck me up, Mac, they'll send me out to that Long Island funny farm with the loonies, the commies—the Jews are out there who wanna steal the atom bomb. I'm a fuckin American, Mac!

Monte, Mac said. It was hard to talk to him, he was beginning to cry. I wouldn't go with nobody but you, Mac, you know that. You'll be OK an tell them, OK? Jus stay there with me a while? Yeah, Monte, yeah. I'll stay. Yeah, they'll let ya stay an then ya walk out. But come back, right, Mac? We'll be inna fuckin cab again inna coupla days goin ta Papa Joe's or someplace, right, Mac? I'll buy ya a thousand beers—take your old lady out too —us guys—us *old* guys gotta stick.

Right.

He was looking out the window again. Where the hell are all the lots, Mac? Member all the fuckin *lots* when we were kids?

I do, Monte.

I'll buy ya a *thousand* beers, Mac. Nothin the matter with you you can't drink beer, right?

Nothin the matter at all, Monte. Mac was dragging diligently on a cigarette. Nothin the matter with you not the matter with all of us, Mac, right.

Right. The cab was rolling smoothly now down Eastern Parkway, catching the synchronized lights.

They give us some fuckin, Mac. I doan know exactly how, but they give us some royal fuckin.

LOFTER
The Colonel Returns

AS A PRIVATE in the Canadian Army, Lofter appeared on the street one day, sweating and red-faced in the heavy, itchy wool uniform, leggings, and stiff hobnailed boots. Clacking and scraping along on the metal heel plates, his arms swinging free in British fashion.

He was changed in that he now had acne. His mother greeted him, it was supposed. Why not? Somebody gotta love the fuck, Artie Salvo said.

What was most strange is that people saw him in that uniform and didn't think it was a uniform—or, they thought it was a uniform . . . but, just a *uniform.* As if he had bought it. It could have been a doorman's uniform, or an usher's. Miss America spat on the sidewalk after him as he swung past her, clicking. Kommando, she said. To her, it was all eastern Europe. Nobody in pants, jacket, and cap that matched boded any good; a simple politics that had preserved her. Nobody cared, or questioned, and the kids waited for him to appear one morning with his army, his broomstick at port arms, prepared to charge.

But he simply walked around, up and down the block, ignoring the ex-members of his corps, having a Coke in Yodel's, a Hershey bar (fingering the oozing pustules on his face), a three-cent vanilla soda. He could have come out of an Army-Navy store. He could have been an extra.

After a week or so, he was gone again, nobody missed him. He had gone to Canada, or England, or Auschwitz, or the Fabian Fox. He was a military man, and had gone where military men go, to some drab destiny, or death. Phil hadn't even recognized him.

Somebody said he'd developed a British accent. Which was, in a small way, a perfection of means. When the war broke out and the older boys were drafted or enlisted, no one ever once thought of them as going to that war in which the Colonel was engaged. His militarism was an accepted fact. The shape of his back, the size of his nose.

1943

CHICKY'S HOUSE

THAT WAS the specific center of the street. Set back from it, old-fashioned, with shady lawn, flowers, umbrella trees—a back yard. The house was stone, two stories and an attic, in the front an iron rail fence set atop a low cement wall. It sat, almost hidden in shadows between Miss America's building and the Metzes'. Everybody sat on the wall in the summer beneath the streetlamp there, holding to the house actually, they felt it going away from them, it would disappear along with the older boys who almost daily went into the service.

Nobody ever saw Chicky's mother. Chicky was believed to be Jewish. She had a large, protruding rump from the beginning. The beginning was all the way back —she had always been there. Her father did not exist. She had no brothers or sisters? She had no friends, even among the older girls. She went in, she went out. The umbrella trees blossomed and put forth their enormous leaves. Some man came in a truck and took care of them, and the rest of the grounds, cut the hedges. Nobody ever chased any of the kids away. Chicky never greeted anybody. She'd walk out, down the steps, along the path, down another flight, open the iron gate. Clang. She'd walk through them toward either avenue, pulling her big buttocks after her. A kind of bitched classic face, a clear line to the nose and delicate cheekbones.

It was the center of the block. They held to it. There were some other old houses thereon, but they had nothing. Boarders and roomers. (Chicky was a roomer?) The very old, the sons and daughters of whom came on Easter and Christmas. They sat on their porches behind the *Brooklyn Eagle.* Their dogs yapped incessantly at the loud summer games, through the long evenings. Chicky's house alone had the sense of the real, and the disappearing. To disappear. It will disappear. It will have disappeared. Chicky grew older and this year, midway through the war: grew up.

She grew breasts. They were large and solid as her ass, overnight. It was a dark Hebraic miracle! She was *seen* by each boy, treasuring his secret hardon. Her mother, perhaps, behind drapes and shades was seen to be moving about occasionally, nervous. Chicky was with soldiers and sailors, but mostly sailors. They would bring her home on occasion but never come to pick her up. She went out alone, chewing gum, her hair in a light cotton kerchief, or free in the wind. The streetlamp brought the glossy light out of it, so that her whole head glittered. Breasts and sailors, the agitated movement in the house.

News of the first dead from the war. Some guy who lived down the block near Fifth. Ya remember the guy had the police dog? She grew into the war, flourished in glorious, drunken fucking with yokel sailors on their way to the South Pacific to have their balls blown off. The house declined, she grew harder, but loose.

Now she came home on Sundays—or sometimes on Saturdays to spend the whole weekend. Toward the end of the year she married a young electrician's mate and brought him home for a night. Then he went off with Chicky on his arm, down into the subway and out to the Coral Sea. She came back and a week later started with some new sailors, young and blond and stupid, lost in the streets, drunk in the bars, Chicky in their arms, smiling, she lit their cigarettes, she loved them all, she fucked them with delight. She came home. She passed under the streetlight, her hair bright in its rays. The house, a little shabby, set back on its trim lawn. It was the actual center of the block. The boys sat around it as if to prevent its escape.

When they spoke of her, the boys shouted, to a popular tune:

> Won't you tell me, dear
> The size of your brassiere?
> Twenty, thirty, or forty?

—despairing in their adolescence, unused, filled with strength, waiting for the war to come and take them. Let the fucking house fall down. Let it choke in weeds. Let the war snap them away. Make them into sailors. Make her see them.

ZIGGY
The Attack

ZIGGY STOPPED for the light in his milk truck. He looked down Fourth Avenue at the sun dazzling off the cars before him and felt the sweat running down his cheeks from out of his hair, so he took his cap off and wiped his sleeve across his face and eyes. When he looked up again he could see them coming, about twenty of them, Germans, moving quietly and very low to the ground, heavy and methodical in their long gray overcoats. He started firing as they got to the top of the little wall about twenty yards in front of the farmhouse. The .30 caliber gun smelled of oil, a crisp smell, he had worked on it all morning, cleaning and oiling it, taking advantage of the lull in the sector. Now they were coming, but it was impossible for them to get over the wall.

One got to the top with both feet scrambling and scraping, his face was red, a drunkard's face, and his jowls were heavy and black-bearded. Ziggy held him for a moment in the sights and then blew him apart—then slugs started to chew the door frame up and he looked to the right. There was a German machine gun down the slope of the hill, with a clear field of fire to his position and they were chopping the farmhouse to pieces, working the fusillade lower as they corrected from his bursts.

The cars were blowing their horns, Ziggy started, the sweat running faster now, he looked to the right, the auto showroom, the shining new models, lights and sun off them, glints of fire. He swung the truck toward them, gunning the engine and pulling out of the road, over the curb, a man looked at him, his mouth open, then jumped out of the way.

Ziggy heard the glass smash, saw the windshield shatter and the truck went over and through the concrete and brick debris, the nickel molding at the baseboard crunching and twisting under the wheels. He stepped down as hard as he could on the gas and the truck ground into a new yellow convertible, shuddered, and rode halfway up the fender, then abruptly flopped over on its side, the bottles all breaking, gallons of milk flowing over the showroom floor, a white river, Ziggy under the truck, bleeding into the milk running around him as it sluiced out of the rear doors. But alive! Alive! He heard the shouts, the loud voices, saw faces over his. They would take him prisoner, good, he would be out of it at last.

1946

BIG STOOP
A Daily Voyage

EVERY DAY he would come out of the house about noon or a little after. At first the little kids would laugh, and the older guys would gape, but later they simply wouldn't look. Down the cellarway he'd go, up again with a tricycle. He'd set it on the street in front of his house. His younger brother would come out and just look at him as he settled himself on the seat, his bony knees sticking out, his feet—the sides, actually, of his feet—on the pedals. Then he'd start off slowly, go a few yards and make an abrupt turn to the right, head for the curb and bump down into the gutter, then straighten the tricycle out and head down the street. He didn't care at all about the traffic.

He'd head straight down 68th past Fourth Avenue to Third, turn left and follow the old trolley tracks down to Papa Joe's, turn again toward the curb and roll into it, bumping against it. Then he'd get off the tricycle and take it into the bar, carrying it under one arm, put it carefully on the bar and chain it with a single loop to one of the beer taps. He didn't remember any of the other guys in the bar, hanging around on 52-20. He'd drink his beer and once in a while say something like Hard right rudder, or Full astern, or something like that, some nautical command. Both of his older brothers were dead and he was almost dead. The bartender let him do what he wanted, he wasn't violent, and they were just waiting for room in the Vets' Hospital so that he could go away forever. He had won the Navy Cross, was the story in Papa Joe's, but everybody lied about everything in there.

1946

LONG WALKS, SILENCES
Mac & Friend

WALK THROUGH THE SNOW. Sit in the park. The bitter cold. The two of them, wordless. Walking in the dark streets, barking of dogs, snow falling from high branches, silver, dazzling in the streetlamps. The crunch of their footsteps, cats moving between cars.

Black Mac had got trenchfoot at Bastogne, the cold

and wet sometimes made his feet sweat and hurt. But it was some dim remembering of waste and terror that hurt him more. Paulie Camden would throw pebbles at the window of the frame house where Mac lived with his young wife and in-laws. Call softly. The figure stark against the snow. Sometimes it would be summer or another season, or a dry, clear winter night. Mac would always see him against snow. A dead man. Another dead man. Jeanette woke at times, angry instantly, Mac putting his clothes on. Go ta bed with *him* tomorrow night! Tell *him* ta cook! She would begin to cry, Mac putting on his clothes.

They would walk, wordless. Paulie limping a little, favoring the leg full of steel splinters. They would sit and smoke, nothing to say, what was there to say? Mac thought of Jeanette, wanted her, wanted to be with her, home, warm, but was here. It was better here. The faces of the dead were closer, more human. Sometimes he would start, hearing the exact intonation of a voice, its inflection, rise, the elegant timbre of laughter.

Why Paulie was with him, Mac did not know, nor did Paulie himself. He really didn't know Mac, they weren't friends. Mac ran around with all the 52-20 madmen in Papa Joe's, Paul with no one in particular, sometimes with one crowd, sometimes another. They both drank too much. Paul a bachelor, Mac had married, somehow, a wartime romance, suddenly, out of the Army and married, no job. The fights were vicious with his in-laws and Jeanette, but what was there to do. They were dead, there were so many dead, just to come back and start in on some desk job, hustle freight, as if that clear, edged laughter never existed?

They sat, the wind blew hard against them, they looked out across the bay from the ridge in Bliss Park. The fat ferries all lights moving to and from Staten Island, sometimes a liner ablaze steaming toward the open sea. Once they heard music, strange. Over the waters, on the faintest breeze, a dance tune, a standard, the liner moving toward Europe and the putrid corpses.

1948

THE INFANTRYMEN

GUS MAKAROS and Joe Kane were breaking the air into small pieces with their guffawing, some story about Joe getting grass stains on the knees of his new suit in the park with a girl who thought she'd get pregnant if she blew him. Laugh. Gus chewed on his cigar, his enormous eagle nose rubbing against it as he laughed, Joe's voice the kind you hear from the bleachers. Ziggy stood, leaning back lightly against the plate-glass window, a restless bunch flowed in and out of Yodel's.

Joe Cornell walked up, in his uniform. He was wearing blue plastic plates under his brass, an infantry-blue ascot, his khakis bloused over jump boots. Over his left pocket were the range medals, bars for various weapons, a Good Conduct ribbon, a combat infantryman's badge. He smiled, in a kind of superior way, offhand. The trooper. Gus waved at him, then Joe Kane, somebody came out of Yodel's and shook his hand. Ziggy was looking at his left pocket.

What's that badge, Joe? You a combat soldier? Where were you a combat soldier? Dint you just go in the Army a coupla years ago? He's been fightin the battle a the whorehouse, Gus said. Laugh. He and Joe broke up again, stamping their feet. Dint you just go in the Army a coupla years ago? Ziggy said again. Joe was looking at him, the creep. Everybody knew he was just out of Pilgrim State after that milk truck scene. Ah, Joe said. He cut the air in front of him with his hand, moving it downward swiftly. They *train* ya now for combat, advanced training, specialized training, weapons specialization . . . when ya finish you're a *combat* infantryman, you don't gotta go in no fuckin mudholes just to prove anything . . . you gotta have it *here,* tapping his forehead. Fight anywhere, anytime, anyway. Ziggy was staring at the badge, the silver was very bright in the hard light from the store. Donato came out. Hey, Joe, heyyy, looka the soljer, looka this sharp stud. Makes me thinka the good ole days in Japan. Lotsa broads, hah, Joe? Lotsa broads there, hah? Since he had been in Japan while in the Army, to Donato, everybody had been in Japan. His head wasn't quite right since the New Year's Eve a Japanese freight had hit a truck that he and six others, soldiers and whores, had been riding in. They were all killed, but he lived. He would tell the story occasionally, laughing about it. Hey, Joe, hah? Japan, hah? He socked Joe's shoulder lightly.

Joe shook the tap off, looking at Ziggy. Whatsamatter? You think I don't deserve this badge? What bug's up your ass? C'mon, c'mon, what's bitin ya? Ziggy had a subtly vacant look on his face, he was looking across the street and giggling, sweating now. Over the wall, he said, I was point gun, over the wall, two other guns behind me, onna left an right. We had beer cans with pebbles in em strung on the wire, but they just came in, fast, fuck the noise. They all died, or got hit, we all got hit, they would come so fast, to take the guns, quick. I'm German, too, I'd think, they'd sure shit themselves if they knew it was me blowin their fuckin guts out. He saw Joe again, and lifted his arm, the hand balled into a club. Combat Infantry-*mun!* Joe backed toward Gus and Joe Kane, the guy was out of his mind! Hey, Joe said, hey, Ziggy, you better go back to the laughin farm . . . hey . . .

I had a fuckin BAR, Gus said, his mouth cracked open in an enormous crescent grin, lotta fuckin good it did me, Makaros, they said, Makaros, if you squeeze off more'n one round at a time from that fuckin weapon they'll know you're the AR an they won't rest till you're dead as shit, so I had the same thing as a fuckin rifle, except it weighed twenty-five pounds, you could get your ass buried in mud under the fuckin thing. Hey, Ziggy, right? You carried an AR for a while? You told me? Joe Cornell had turned and was walking quickly toward the Royal. Hey, Zig, you got shafted with a good ole AR, dint ya? Ziggy was staring after Joe, his arm stiff at his side, the fist still cramped, then he smiled at Gus. Oh, Gus, that damn AR! Were you an AR man the whole route? Shit, yes! Joe Kane was breaking up, banging his palm against the lamppost.

1946

MONTE THE COUNT
The Baptism

McGINN LEANED, drunk, against the bar in Lento's. His right eye was swollen shut where a cop had laid a nightstick across his face two nights before. Under and around the metal plate in his head there was an unwavering current of sharp pain that wouldn't stop, that, in fact, the liquor seemed to intensify. I should be dead, he thought. I should be dead far away from here, far away, O far away . . . she loved him in the springtime and he's far far away, he sang, and downed his shot. Black Mac turned to look at him. Have another John, he said, I got some money, have another.

McGinn rubbed at his swollen eye tenderly and moved his hand up to the cold, shiny surface of the plate covering his brain. My head hurts me, Mac, he said. Jesus, I mean it hurts me terrible. Ah, ya fuck, ya got all that disability money comin soon for the resta ya life. You got it by the balls. He signaled the bartender for two more boilermakers, then turned to continue talking with Ziggy.

It was red in front of McGinn's eyes after he had drunk the whiskey. He retched, then calmed, then retched again, but finally kept the shot down. Then he very carefully set the shot glass down, picked up his beer and drank it all slowly. As he was setting the beer glass down, it got very red. He looked at Mac and saw him as if he were looking at him through a piece of red cellophane. Like when they were all kids before the war, looking at the green park through the cellophane, the new world, intense, red and weird before them. It was silent, he saw everybody's mouth moving but he could only hear the jukebox, clear, day clear, the mouths, the movement of the men at the bar, Frank the bartender drawing two beers. The pain in his head was down in his ears now, in his neck, clean and sharp into the swollen eye. I should be dead.

He was standing on the bar now, surprised to find himself there and the noise of the saloon came back. The pain in his head was gone and he saw them all clearly, they had sent him to the war. You bastards! he shouted, you bastards! You ain't got a plate in your head! Mac was touching, gently, his ankle, motioning with his head for him to get down, and Frank was drying his hands patiently, giving McGinn time to get down by himself. A good kid he was, got hurt a little in the war but a good kid.

You bastards, McGinn shouted. The bar was dead quiet now, the jukebox stopped, the customers watching him standing there, high above them. He lifted his hand up over his head, gloriously, and saw himself, outside himself, above them all, the men of the king's guard, McGinn in a cloak, soft boots, a rapier elegant, pointed straight up. He raised his hand high. I am the Count of Monte Cristo! he shouted, I am the Count of Monte Cristo! He kicked at Mac's drink and smashed it to the floor, then kicked at the glasses next to him on the bar, hearing them break, shouting through the absolute clarity now in his head, I am the Count of Monte Cristo! You bastards, you sent the Count to the war! He was screaming now, and someone at the far end of the bar started for the door. Hold it, you bastard! Hold it! You ain't callin no bulls on me! The man stopped, shrugged, walked back to the bar. Frank began moving quietly and casually down toward McGinn, smiling sickly. I am the Count! I am the Count, he was crying now, weeping freely, his arms at his side, the pain back in his head, his eye, his ears, the bar had gone silent to him, there were movements, feet scuffling, he saw them through the tears, out there they moved through their lives in dead silence, I am the Count of Monte Cristo, you mothers' cunts! he screamed, the tears running down his face, dropping down on his faded fatigue jacket, dark stains spreading on its front as Mac and Frank helped him to the floor.

1945

THE SAILORS

THEY'D WANTED to steal a couple of cartons of heavy plaid shirts to peddle to the truck drivers and longshoremen on the waterfront, but someone—or all of them—

got frightened at a noise inside the Army-Navy store and they ran with whatever they could take. Konik and Fat Phil wound up with two gross each of blue felt bedroom slippers, but Frank Bull got two cartons with navy whites; jumpers in one, and bell bottoms in the other. They would masquerade.

The last year of the war, Germany defeated, the machine was rolling, the Japanese being ground to pieces. Everyone was bored, and tired of it. The sailors, the soldiers, no one cared a damn about them, one way or the other. They would reel around the streets, up out of the subway, drunk, looking for Times Square and Greenwich Village, ending up arrested by the MP's from Fort Hamilton, lost yokels.

They would masquerade. Frank and Konik and Phil, sailors for a night, they'd go drinking down by the Navy Yard and see what happened—maybe they could roll some sailors, they'd get to be pals with them, buy some goddam ribbons and chevrons, any damn thing, come on like John Wayne, roll the swabbies' asses. Or at least have some laughs, maybe get laid.

The trio. Ill-fitting whites, the campaign ribbons, some Army decorations among them, pinned on crooked, too high on the breast. Konik had black wing-tip shoes on, no hat. They didn't care. Eddy and the Doc saw them getting into a taxi outside the Lion's Den, but they didn't even mention it. They weren't even sure whether the three were really in the Navy or not. Who cared? Swabby bastards.

A convoy must have just gone out because the bars were almost empty of sailors. They drank, using twenty dollars they'd pooled to start with. After the twenty, they'd use whatever money they had themselves. But the barmaid swallowed their lies, and so did some fat riveter from the Yard, guilty over his thirty-hours-a-week overtime. So they got drunk, no rollings, no girls.

They moved from bar to bar, into cabs and out, Frank making up the stories about Bataan and Wake Island, Midway, anything that came to his head. The Seabees. The Fighting Seabees! Goddammit! Kill the fuckin Jap basteds an Joo basteds too, Frank yelled, they better watch their fuckin step!

They were in Sunset Park and reeling around, singing, pissing into trash cans. On a bench there was a skinny Italian kid with a girl. Looka this! Frank said. Konik and Phil wanted to get a cab and go to the Royal, but Frank stood there, the booze running through his brain, looking at the kid and the girl, Phil pulling at his sleeve. The girl was terrified, and kept half-getting up, but the kid sat very still, looking at Frank. You're a fuckin 4-F Joo basted, Frank said. You're sitting here fuckin with all these whores, makin plenty a money, while us guys—he flung his arms toward Europe and Japan—get our asses blown off! Well, I'm gonna straighten you out!

Konik and Phil stood, frightened. Frank had placed himself swiftly and precisely into a murderous mood, at this moment he *was* a sailor, a hero-sailor, who had been grievously wounded, his best buddies blasted by sneaking, fanatic kamikazes. Frank hit the kid across the face. You mocky basted! and the kid got up and started to run, the girl sitting there, her hands grinding in her lap. The kid couldn't run so well, he had a slight gimp, and Frank was right on him. As he turned him around and hit him with a huge fist, Konik and Phil began to run the other way, the girl sitting, immobile. The sound of Frank's fists hitting the kid again, and then again, were very clear in the calm air. At the exit to the park they stopped and looked back, thought they heard Frank's voice, harsh, but they weren't sure. I hope ta Christ the broad makes a run for it, Konik said, I just hope ta Christ. Phil looked at this strange drunken figure, his friend, in dirty whites, this sailor, then down at his own body, the multicolored ribbons at the corner of his eye, very bright in the streetlight. He unpinned the top row: a Silver Star and a Purple Heart, and threw them into the black grass. Take those fuckin things off, Konik, for Jesus' sake, take em *off!* He turned and walked out of the park, unfastening the second row: Good Conduct, European Theater, Pacific Theater with three Battle Stars.

1943

PAT GLADE
Pretty Bobby Shaftoe

IT WAS THE FOOD? It was that he was afraid of the water? (For a sailor!) Or just that he couldn't learn to swim? Maybe he wanted his mama?

He was back on the corner, hardly away when he was back, in blues, from Great Lakes. Was this the flashy second baseman? Was this the kid who thought anybody who went to public school was a dirty Protestant? He was back, in the blues, then out of the blues, then all of a sudden playing softball again, surehanded as usual around the keystone.

Gibby watched him boxing, stand-up Irish style that black men had already made obsolete: graceful. Patsy used to make fun of his shorts and long wool stockings and that his mother was on relief. "The relief" he called it. Dirty. Pushing a very sharp and accurate left into Doc's face, and hooking off it nicely. Back from the mess hall. From boot. Back to the streets with his discharge safe. He served. His mother with her blue star banner, faded in the sun, in the window, yapping about the 4-F Jews, Patsy dancing straight up, his head rocking from side to side, the light off those auburn curls. He served. Right! Jab, jab, hook the head, hook the body, cross.

1945

FAT PAREZ
Fort Hamilton

BRING your batt-aliowns to att-enshun!

Batt-AL-iowns! Tenn-SHUN!

Bitter wind, driving harsh sleet in it occasionally. The officers and attendant civilians in the reviewing stand straight in the cold, shivering.

". . . William Leonard Parez, Private First Class, United States Army . . . in and on the outskirts of the village of . . . at great risk to his personal safety repeatedly rallied his platoon after both his commanding officer and . . . utter disregard for . . . succeeded in destroying a machine-gun emplacement which had . . . though mortally wounded . . . his commanding officer and two men of his . . . refused medical attention . . . this Silver Star is posthumously awarded."

Bring your batt-aliowns to pa-rade rest!

Batt-AL-iowns! Pa-VADE HEST!

The sleet harder, rattling off the lacquered helmet liners.

Bring your batt-aliowns to att-enshun!

Batt-AL-iowns! Tenn-SHUN!

Trumpets, retreat, the flag folded in the icy twilight. Fuck *this* shit, a trooper mutters, Jesus!

PASS IN REVIEWW!

Oh! The monkey wrapped his tail
Around the flagpole . . .

Move em *out,* you motherfuckers.

1945

THE BOMB

THAT DID IT. The *News* had pictures showing how New York would be affected if they dropped one on 42nd Street. A lotta shit. Those places were all made of grass, New York would have a little damage, that's all. Then it was over, they gave up and it was over.

Some of the boys, sixteen and seventeen, were very annoyed that the whole thing ended before they ever got a chance to get into it. Kill some barbarians, get some good nookie. Make a man out of you, their machinist fathers said. I remember in the artillery. Once in the infantry. In France, on leave, in Paris—well, I'll tell you when you get a little older. Ha ha. Good old days. Let the dead bury the dead.

They reaped the whirlwind. Right? They could have given up long ago. Right? Nobody wants to kill innocent civilians but they were all in on it. Look at the Death March. Look at Bataan. Look at Corregidor. Look at Wake Island. Look at Tarawa. Look at PEARL HARBOR! You son of a bitches! Now just look at Pearl Harbor! Dot dot dot dash. V for Victory. They'd have killed everybody in sight. Yellow Nazis.

Some of the boys worried about their friends and brothers coming back with medals and stories. They'd have to listen to them and lie about all the cunt they'd been getting. A forced smile into the hard faces of these young warriors, their resplendent ribbons and brass.

We would have never given up if they dropped it here. It shows how chickenshit the nip bastards were. Fuck up a coupla cities and they quit. That's why America is great. Great America. All hail America! The drunken heroes would be back soon, glittering in their boots under flags and with the regimental bands playing. They'd lie to them about the lousy meat. How they smoked Chelseas and Rameses. You couldn't get any butter at all. You guys had it knocked. The Good Army life. You bet.

The bomb did it all. Everybody could have had a chance to get into it if it hadn't been for the fuckin bomb.

They were on the way back now. Strange. Heaps of charred arms and legs, ripped genitals and shattered brains between them and the quarreling lines waiting to buy chuck chopped.

1951

MONTE THE COUNT
The Last Stand

AFTER HE SMASHED Papa Joe's window with his cast, he stood for a moment, then, very wisely, walked rapidly down the block toward the bay. It would take a while for the cops to come, he'd sit in some driveway till morning, then just go down to the ferry and ride back and forth a while. It was almost five anyway. But he stopped in the middle of the block and started back, stood then on Papa Joe's corner and watched the prowl car coming down Third Avenue, slow to a halt. The first cop got out, swinging his nightstick, grinning at him. Monte walked over slowly, humbly, then when he got to within a few feet of the cop, kicked him in the balls. He fell backward, and Monte smashed him across the skull with the cast. Then he ran around to the driver's side as the cop was getting out there, the door just about a foot open, the cop's foot grazing the street. Monte kicked at the door with all his strength, slamming the cop's ankle between it and the car frame. He saw the cop's face go white and he started to laugh. The cop drew his gun and leveled it at Monte, pushed the door all the way open, his nightstick high over his shoulder in his other hand. Monte drew the cast back to paste him and the cop put the stick across the side of his head and laid him out. He sat in the open door of the car, the gun still trained on him, thinking about firing.

1941

GHOST SHIPS

THE RUMOR was that they were inhabited by hundreds of giant water rats. They swam through the filthy waters of the bay, their greasy, vicious heads held above the rotting orange peels and condoms. Their yellow teeth.

They were about a half-mile from the ferry slips, in a small cove that accepted the sewage from a huge pipe that jutted, brown with rust and shit, out into the water. Half-sunk and rotted, wooden hulls and superstructure, three of them. Never painted or fitted out, they were not yet completed when the Armistice was signed in 1918, someone had launched them. They were there, awash, swarming with the garbage-fat rats.

They were to be destroyed as targets by the Navy. They were to be repaired and used as ferry boats. They were to be sunk as breakwaters up at Hell Gate. They were to rot forever.

The rats were bigger than dogs and could chew your arm off. They'd killed at least two kids who went swimming years ago. They spoke in tongues. The gypsies caught them and ate them. They were what they made bubble gum from, and glue. They came on shore all together once every ten years. Don't go near the water's edge at night. At full moon.

The ships huddled and sometimes changed position in storms. No troops had ever boarded them, but Big Mickey had heard someone call to him one gray afternoon from the empty decks. They wallowed in the tides.

There were men, alive, in the neighborhood, married, with children, who had been scheduled to sail into death on these ships. They didn't know who they were. At sunset they would glow red in the last pink rays from Jersey. Ghosts and rats.

The war had ended without them. They groaned in the mud, the rotten wood splintering and crackling, falling in pieces into the water.

It was said that every year at midnight of Armistice Day you could hear the satanic shrieking of the rats. In tongues, calling for blood.

1943

DANCING IN THE DARK

THEY WERE the leaders of the block now. All the older ones gone, or turning into drunks. They had dances all over that year, it was a beginning to ease juvenile delinquency, gang rumbles, V-girls. There were church dances, teen canteens, dances at the K of C. On Senator

Street, the boys came after the girls in technique. It was the girls who taught them.

They learned in the cellars. The floors swept, emery dust over the cement, some bottles of ginger ale and Pepsi, and some of the boys with beer and wine, slouching in their drapes and turned-up collars against the walls. Dancing to the Duke, Tommy Dorsey, Harry James, Count Basie, Erskine Hawkins, Glenn Miller, Glen Gray. The light bulbs strung, hanging over the walls of the coal bin, the portable record player, and they learned the steps from the girls.

To see them in the gloomy cellars, dancing in the winter evenings. The girls in their good dresses, and the boys in sharp chalk stripes from Buddy Lee's and Ripley's, drapes from Obie's, suede shoes sliding over the floor in slow, easy Lambeth Walk. The Glen Island Dip, trucking and lindying, the youth coming out of them clear and sharp, putting away their childhood forever.

That stunning sweetness of the girls, those boring girls that each boy had tormented and chased for years, there they were. In their Sunday dresses, the thin sweetness of the sweat smell from them, mixed with a first perfume. Their young bodies, stiff against their own new breasts and widening hips, their soft thighs. The boys held them.

They held them close in foxtrots, swaying gently, rubbing against them, dumb in their lust. The slide of the dress material over their underwear, the lace that swirled out at the hem. That they could be fucked! That they were unbearably female! That they wore brassieres! Helpless before it. Scowling into their cheap cigarettes, moving to the corners of the cellar to slug some Tokay or port. Lizzie and Dolores and Mary. Georgene, Annette, Joyce. Edith and Terry. They crossed their legs, they giggled, they whispered, they danced. Their bodies moved. They floated gently through that sparse light. Their brothers were killing. Their fathers were working in the Navy Yard. They were to be women, inexorable toward that state.

The boys fell in love, they fell out of love, they insulted these girls who set them in a rage of lust and longing. The smell of perfume. The cold air off their clothes as they came in from the evening. The insanely delicious taste of forbidden cigarettes. The blushes of the girls who were cut in on. Rage, the boys fell apart in desire.

They would never chase them again. They would never play street games with them again. They had smelled the woman in them. They looked and needed. Who were these strange women? Where had they been? Dancing in the gloom, in the dark, disappearing in couples into the back of the cellar, what is this? What is happening? Who are these remote women! Smell of first perfume from them, lacy underwear covering their secret bodies, the clear odor of sweat, to be worshipped, to be knelt before with tears and grunts of anguished lechery. The absolute end of childhood, there dancing.

1937

68th STREET
The Gypsy's Hand

IN THE HOT NIGHTS, ghost stories. Sitting, seven or eight boys, in a circle, next to Flynn's Tavern, outside a doorway opening onto a flight of steep, narrow stairs, one dim bulb at the top: down from which could come monsters, fiends of any visage! The noise of the street excluded, sealed off from this magic ring. The Gypsy's Hand, told and told again, embellished and refined, honed to a perfect tool to construct fear.

The Gypsy, his hand severed so that he could never play his violin again. There in his clearing, next to the campfire, the garish caravan about. And what was it that destroyed him, killed him, tore his hand from his body? Somewhere there were tourist Americans, locked into the narrative. A car had done it, some heavy, shining gadget or other. They impinged on his life, at all events, tore him from the land, his sweet meadows, battering his culture. A man in a Tyrolean with red feather, some bland-faced woman in white, relaxing beside him on the soft leather of the Rolls touring car. The quaint, delightful Gypsy! And the mountains in the distance. Ah God, incredible.

Died and his hand torn off. Which returned to take its revenge. Garrotting and clawing, punching out of eyes. The boys sat, cold and alone on the hot streeet, the drunks reeling out of Flynn's, down the stairs the almost palpable configurations of alien monsters, gaunt, twisted in hatred and lust for revenge, speaking garbled foreign tongues dark in their mouths.

1936

JOE CORK & JERRY SMYTHE

THEIR REAL NAMES, two Irish kids, who did not live on the block—any block, but on Fifth Avenue, so had no territory at all to inhabit. Their mothers both alone, both on relief. Joe lived over a candy store in a small apartment looking out on the trolley car tracks. Jerry over Fritz's Tavern, a few blocks down the avenue. They knew each other from school, from the free lunches, and knew some kids on 68th—it became their block. Joe was kind and stupid, Jerry very bright, but reserved. Cold. At first they came around together, but then Jerry came either earlier or later than Joe. They played with the regular street gang, got to know them all.

A particular pattern of loneliness, who knows about it? That it could wrench your guts, their mothers in their broken shoes, sopping in the snow, the kids in their sopping threadbare knickers, their runny noses, dancing with grace among the others, in the slush, shrieking. Camaraderie of the depression! They didn't know they were poor! Stick it up your ass, gentle *lecteur!* Joe and Jerry, Joe and Jerry, Joe and Jerry, a few blocks from the ferry, making greaty merry! Slow and thickwitted, ah, bright and clear-eyed, gray-eyed, the two gifts to the block that needed their, ah, "color." Right?

Inexorably toward the trucks, old Joe, the trucks and the Army and the trucks again, who knows, just another one: flat red hair. The other, silent Jerry, toward the priesthood? A Jesuit, if anything. Do you give a fuck? Let them stand there, frozen in snapshot: "City Fun"— soaking cheap cardboard shoes, their bellies full of stale bread and canned milk. Making of Americans! Got it?

1935

MERRY XMAS
Tin Pig

LITTLE MICKEY'S MOTHER was dancing around the living room, holding an imaginary partner in her arms, singing drunkenly, When they begin the beguine, It brings back a night of tropical splendor, It brings back a memory so tender, It brings back a night of tropical splendor —Oh, let them begin the beguine, let them begin. She was really stewed, a half quart of Three Feathers standing on top of the Philco radio. It was about 2 A.M.

Little Mickey watched her from the bedroom, waiting for her to go to bed so that Santa could come and bring him the sled and the other stuff he wrote him for. Santa couldn't come if anyone was up, she told him that. He knew, remotely, that she would like to be over in Flynn's with her friends, and felt blue about that, but she was good, she was good. She was dancing and looked kind of nice.

The tin pig was under the tree, with a blue jacket and sailor cap, a little red drum that he beat, hopping on the linoleum when he was wound up. But Mickey had seen his mother put that under the tree, so it had nothing to do with Christmas. Your mother didn't have to give you anything for Christmas, Santa did all that. He kept watching her, his eyes burning. He wished, really, that she'd go to bed.

He fell asleep and when he woke saw her lying on the couch. The bottle was empty and under the little artificial tree he saw the pig, still alone. But the lamplight in the room was pale and weak and then he realized that the dawn had come. And then he knew. There was no Santa, nobody like Santa. He never came and never would.

He was a sweet and generous child. There was nobody to blame, it was all some story that grown-ups had about things. Unless he just didn't leave him anything? But he knew that there was none, no Santa.

Didn't want to see anybody else's anything! And wouldn't wind that tin pig up, ever. The pig grinned under the tree, the gray bitter light falling across his red epaulets.

Just before he'd fallen asleep, she'd really been dancing! He remembered her now, spinning, and gliding, holding the bottle by the neck, smiling and stretching her hand out to the air: A night of tropical splendor. A night of tropical splendor. Let them play. She looked really good dancing, really pretty. His sudden acceptance of her sorrow.

1935

THE OLD WITCH

THEY LIVED on the ground floor, so little Jake would run in off the street dozens of times a day. A glass of water, a glass of milk, tie my shoes, dry gloves, nobody to play with, the kids were hitting him, in and out. His mother, abandoned for three years by the father, poor and on relief, struggling with her misery and loneliness, watching him, trying hard to keep her temper. Her one child, a beloved boy, but he demanded, and demanded. After school, in and out, all day Saturday, all summer, and this year worse then ever, nervous and worried on the new block. Play with the other kids! That little Artie kid, Gibby what's his name, play with that nice kid Charlie Taylor and his sister.

And he did, but it was easy to run in, push open the door, and ask, or whine, or slouch and lounge and fall on the floor, roll around with the cat.

His mother at the sink, washing out some things, in pink rayon step-ins and rolled silk stockings, no brassiere. Jake ran in, a glass of water. A glassa water, Ma? He looked at her, she was strange, her heavy breasts that he had never seen, her body clear and real before him. She stood, her hands dripping suds, struck shamefaced and shamed at being such. Lonely body. It was still youthful and desirable, she felt her own sexuality raging underneath her clothes, in the store, at mass, at night, twisted into her bunched nightgown. The boy was looking at her and she felt the shame, the rage, he was looking at her, assaulting her privacy, lonely and bitterly held together by a bitter sense of morals. He was looking at her.

She wanted to cover her crotch, then her breasts, she stood with the socks in her hands, red-faced. Caught by her little boy, caught as woman. Felt herself redden more, turn stone toward her son. Dirty! she said, Dirty! Get out of here! Dirty! Filthy! He was gone, upset and in fear, it wasn't his mother—there was nothing he could recognize, this strange woman violently angry. In her flesh. He went out into the cold wind of the street.

But came back fifteen minutes later. Days later for him. As she knew he would. And had decided to punish him the moment he had first left. She stood in the bathroom, the door locked. It wasn't dirty. He wasn't dirty, not really, a little boy, six years old. But he had to learn, he *had* to learn to stop running in and out of the house a million times a day, she'd have to teach him a lesson. Felt her body assaulted beneath the house dress she'd put on. It was naughty, that's right. Naughty, probably got it from those little bastards on the street to look at his mother. But she'd teach him a lesson—about running in and out. He was only a little boy, six. Felt assaulted and stared at, a dirty dream. Dirty! Dirty! And had had some. And had thought of things her husband had tried to do. Dirty!

When Jake came in this time he stopped short, looking for her, then called, and called again. She knocked at the bathroom door from inside. Jake, she called, and was thrilled, to play a game, a trick, so clearly in command. Jake, she called. Who's there, who's that, where's my mommy? Your mommy had to go out, Jake, I'm the old witch and your mommy told me to tell you to stop running in and out of the house. The old witch don't like that.

She spoke these words in her own voice, absolutely undisguised. And the child heard them as terrifying, strange sounds, unrecognizable. It was the old witch! He fell on the floor in terror and hysterics. His mother rushed from the bathroom when she heard the whine, the animal sounds from him, and snatched him into her arms, It's me, Jakie, it's Mama, Jakie! There was no old witch, it was a game, Mama was playing a game, but he persisted for an hour, two hours, and finally calmed enough to be put to bed, with her next to him, holding his hand, tears dropping from her eyes. The terrified child twitching in his sleep so that she then got into bed with him, wrenched and sick, lost, holding this dear child close, bitter and confused.

In the night he woke and whispered to her, Mama, is the old witch gone? Is she gone? And she said, There was no witch, baby, weeping openly now, there was no witch, baby, Mama was playing a trick on you. Is the old witch gone, Mama? She's gone, Jakie. She's gone, yes.

And for weeks after he would not go into the bathroom nor pass its door without her. And thought of her being sent away somewhere that terrible day in her underpants, her strange full breasts naked to everyone.

1936

THE ACCIDENT

PAT WAS in his Our Lady of Angels school uniform, navy blue knickers, black shoes and socks, white shirt, blue tie. His schoolbag swung from his hand, bulging with those special Catholic texts, catechisms, cards decorated with Jesus and Mary, weird bleeding hearts, dripping bloody crowns of thorns. Dago, he said to Gibby, you're a Protestant Dago. Not, Gibby said, looking at Pat, bigger, older by three or four years. And he was born on this block. His block. Not? Pat said, not a wop? Not a Protestant, Gibby said. But a wop, Pat said. An American, Gibby said, he fumbled, Amerc-ican, like you. I'm *Irish,* Pat said. My mother's Irish, Gibby said. Your mother's on the relief.

"The" relief, he called it. The article specifically making it shameful. Depraved, like people who didn't go to O.L.A. You're no Catholic, Pat said. You don't go to no Catholic school, you go to the Public School with the Jews and Protestants.

You're a thick mick, Gibby said. You look like hell in those clothes, he said, and ran, Pat after him, the schoolbag swinging. Gibby ran up his stoop and into the hall, slammed the door behind him and Pat put his hand right through one of the panes of glass. The blood ran out and onto his white shirt, oozed down the glass and his face went white. As did Gibby's. But what sweetness. To savor that look, to remember it for years, that cherub face, the curls, the small nose, clear skin. The mind filled with sewage laced through with fear. Pat ran down the stoop and toward his own house, his arm held away from his side, the blood trailing. In a pig's ass Protestant, in a pig's ass, Gibby yelled after him, shaking and excited. He'd go to jail, Cockroach would put him in jail, he was Irish too. In a pig's ass, he yelled again. Thick mick, he said.

PAT GLADE
Good, Steady Job

AT WORK: in a drawer, a fifth of rye.

In the men's room, under some rags on top of a water tank, another.

In an old galosh in the mop closet, a pint of Old Mr. Boston Orange-Flavored Gin.

Thus did our . . .

make it through the day.

The mornings were the worst. He had a cab, paid for by the week, to pick him up outside Gallagher's every morning at nine. He'd get to the bar by eight thirty and have a few doubles and a beer and smoke a couple of cigarettes, then the driver would honk and Pat would come out, get in. By the time he was downtown at his desk, he'd be alive.

Now he was an assistant clerk. Good, steady job. Vacation and sick time, and you can't fire the Civil Service, no matter the rye and Mr. Boston.

He'd look out over the buildings and toy with papers, get some booze in him, toy with a pencil, get some booze in him, look out the windows, do a half hour's work and go out to lunch: a sandwich with two or three beers, a couple of shots, with another beer, a shot to get him back the two blocks to the office. Then the afternoon would begin. Onward. Monday over, to the bar, a few, a few more, the subway, up, out, into Gallagher's, a few more, home to his potatoes and mother. A few beers with supper, blanking out, floating away, his mother's voice on and on about the prices, who got drafted, who didn't, the snippy little thing with his fat ass. Looked like a Jew to Mrs. Glade. Pat, gliding away, away. Then out for a paper after a couple of hours of TV, on the corner, almost sober, the great debate, one little one? A short one. One whiskey and one short brew. That's it. Zonked, home, up to his Gallagher's breakfast and cab ride.

On the weekends it never stopped. He talked about how he could have been a great drummer. He meant like Buddy Rich. Bam! Powerhouse! He'd tap with his hands on the various bars to the various jukeboxes, pleasantly enough, in time, smiling. One day he'd take those lessons, and get straightened out. For a guy with his natural sense of rhythm, and beat, and music, it would just be a matter of learning to read for percussion. Right? Right, Patsy, some one or other would say, helping him off the barstool and out to a cab. He figured he could go on forever, why not? No expenses to matter, good, steady job. Cut the shit out any goddam time he fuckin well wanted to. Right? Right, Patsy.

1949

PAT GLADE
Merry Xmas

PAT LEANED OVER THE TUB, looking at the fat roach racing up its far side. Whoozhy, whoozhy. The big cockaroach. He wasn't too drunk, he thought. I am not too drunk, he said. It's Christmas, anyway. A shower, a cold shower, and a beera, two beera, three beera, an then the good fuckin lamb chops, the delicious Irish spuds, cooked by the varicosed hands of my old mother. The roach was gone, into a crack. I coulda drowned the bastard.

Spuds, spuds, boiled, with butter, good Irish cuisine,

great Irish chow! But yes, Mom, I'll be delighted to have another five, six poundsa spuds, put em right there, on the plate, nexta the fuckin chops, nexta the fuckin strings beans. But you wouldn't begrudge me a beer to get the juices flowing? Ah, dear old spalpeen of a mother! Arra! Go on!

He leaned further to turn on the water, loosening his tie. He fell in the tub. In the tub, O Jesus! In the tub. He struggled to get up but it was no use. Fuck it, I'll just take a bath, no shower, a cold bath. A hot bath? To *sweat* the booze out! That's a good idea, room for the Christmas chops, the holiday spuds, then, the strings beans. He threw his tie on the floor. In the tub. Off with the shoes, cordovan wing-tip shoes, the rage this year. He pushed one shoe off, then the other. They lay in the tub, by the drain, and he looked at them. Ah, what the hell. He put the stopper in and ran the hot water, then the cold, adjusted the temperature until it was just right, watching his shoes moving slightly in the water now swirling at his feet. A bath. He laughed. A coupla beers. A rest from Civil Service, a holiday vacation from it all. His pants were soaked, the pockets weighed down with water.

He began to laugh, very loudly. Hey, Ma! He yelled. Hey, Ma, how you like this bath? His mother came to the door and knocked on it. She didn't like to see Pat drunk, not on this holiday, O Jesus, not on Christmas Eve, with his father not home yet. Open it up, Ma! It's not locked! She opened the door and looked at Pat in the tub, the water up around his armpits. Wash and wear, he said. Wash and beer. Oh, Jesus Mary and Joseph! She turned the water off. Get out, Pat! Oh, God help us all, get out!

The front door opened and Mr. Glade came in, reeling against the wall. Chrismas! he said, ah, Chrismas! He smiled and looked at Pat in the tub, Pat looked back at him. Git outa the tub, what's he in the tub, Mary? he said. Mrs. Glade looked at her husband, Pat, she said, you're drunk, you said you'd have one or two, you said one or two this year. Like father, like son, Pat said. Right, Mr. Glade said, but you gotta get outa that tub, Pat, son. Look at that suit! Look out, Mary, he said. He walked into the bathroom past his wife. Pat, sit down a minute, she said. Sit down? Fer wat? Let me git me son outa there.

He reached over and grabbed Pat's arms, and Pat laughed and very calmly pulled him into the tub. He went in slowly, easily, trying to maneuver so that he wouldn't lean too heavily on Pat. They lay in the water, face to face. Put on the spuds, Ma, Pat said. The golden Irish spuds.

1941

FREDO & RED

ONE DAY in early spring, Fredo pulled Red Mulvaney off the Ulmer Park trolley so that he fell on his shoulder and elbow, badly bruising himself. Red had about twenty pounds on Fredo, a large, heavy-boned boy against Fredo's dark, almost girlish body. They were both about twelve.

Fredo hated Red for his very largeness, that blond reddish cast to his complexion, his square jaw, open brutal laugh. He had greenish decaying teeth, square and well-formed but soft and given to rot. Fredo was light brown with blue-black hair and eyes, and perfectly made. He was very tough and never went to school. Never went home either, so far as anyone knew. Red played hooky all the time and always got caught, hated school because he was stupid. Fredo neither liked it nor disliked it. He found the streets more interesting, so he was on the streets. Beginning now to pick up a few dollars stealing from boxcars in the Long Island yards and grabbing change from newsstands. Wherever he wanted to go he'd hitch on a trolley car. It was useful, meaningful transportation for his busy life. Red hitched for fun, as did the other boys. But the other boys didn't offend Fredo, it was this Irish son of a bitch, this cop, that got him—he even looked like a cop to Fredo. So this one day he just ran up when the trolley stopped at 69th Street and pulled Red the hell off it.

Red looked at him, smiling, fixed, his shoulder and elbow shot through with pain, smiling and silent. Fredo waited for him to get up so he could fight him, get the whole thing out in the open and simply kick the shit right out of him, kick his ass right there in the street. Or any time. That he should hitch, that act, enraged Fredo, made his own hitching shabby and tawdry, meaningless. Any time he wanted it.

But Red looked and smiled, OK, Fredo, OK. You win, Fredo. He knew why he had been pulled off, clearly. Safe and solid in his heavy flesh he knew that Fredo wanted him to get up so that he could whip him. That hate and contempt were perfect in the air, luminous.

You better watch your fuckin hitchin, Red, Fredo said. On *my* trolleys. This's *my* trolley, I'm goin to Coney. You pay your goddam fare or hitch where I can't see ya—and swung then, loose and gallant, onto the trolley as it started to move, Red rising, rubbing his bruises, looking after him, his face pink with anger, mouth brittle in a smile of bitter hatred. That would persist and flourish.

RED'S GRANDMA

SHE SAT in the broken Morris chair, her leg over one arm so that Red could see up her pale-blue-veined leg to the twisted reddish hairs of her crotch. She squinted through her glasses, the nose piece held together with adhesive tape. She chased him around the dining room table with thin patent leather belts from her crepe de Chine dresses. She rifled the dumbwaiters for yesterday's papers, so that everything they read in that house smelled of garbage. She made head cheese and boiled potatoes for supper once a month. She fried eggs so that the whites were black and elastic and the yolks underdone and scummy. She made toast over the flame of the gas range so that it was charred. She called Red's mother a tramp and his father a bum. She gave her husband enough money for one pack of cigarettes every three days. She unplugged all the lamps at night so that the electricity wouldn't leak out of the walls and raise the light bill. She called everyone shanty Irish or nigger rich. She never kissed her husband. She wore dresses that stank of sweat and were grayly filthy. She used perfume from the five-and-ten. She cut her corns with a fish knife. She saved string and had a drawer full of it hopelessly knotted. She allowed everyone one egg a week. She cooked beans so that they stuck to the bottom of the pot and burned. She never baked cake, pie, rolls, biscuits, or bread. She turned on the radio as Red began his homework. She threw poisoned bread to the sparrows on the adjoining roofs. She had an artificial Christmas tree two feet high with no decorations or lights. She put it on the end table on Christmas Eve and put it back in the closet at nine Christmas night. She lifted her ass off the chair to fart at the table. She drank her coffee and tea out of a saucer. She never went to the movies. She made Red leave the door open when he went to the bathroom. She had never seen her husband's genitals nor ever touched them. She liked to hit Red on the top of the head with her knuckles. She never went to church and feared priests. She had her husband's savings in her name. She had her engagement ring in a safe-deposit vault. She had a patchy fur coat that she wore on New Year's Day. She would not enter a saloon but got beer-drunk every night. She cracked pretzels on her bottom front teeth. She bought fruit and vegetables with rotten spots. She was terrified of cats and dogs. She thought all Italians were monkeys. She crossed herself when she passed a church. She told Red that if he ever went in a Protestant church he'd drop dead on the spot. She was afraid of mail. She never answered the doorbell. She made fun of her husband's frayed ties. She didn't know how to iron. She used strips of old pillowcases to stop her flow. She drank a blended whiskey and ginger-ale high-ball on Christmas Eve. She spoke of her courting days with absolute contempt. She wore no underwear in the house ever. She thought the superintendent was a Jew because he was flatfooted. She called Red a pimp when she was angry with him. She put on a false girlish voice when she talked to the landlord. She ate mustard sand-wiches and belched with her mouth wide open. She wore a crystal-and-diamond lavaliere when she went to the bank. She had a subtle odor of feces about her. She had frightening dreams about nuns. She saved Red from an orphanage. Dirty old cunt.

SPRENGER
The Silver Screen, &c.

HIS FATHER looked like him, grown fat and old and balding. His mother looked exactly like his father, with a wiglike topping of straw hair, light brown and patchy blond. Both of them missing the bottom front teeth, and they chain-smoked, the mother never puffing. Her cigarette dangled. One sister's face—the one home from the hospital for the holidays—was obscured when in company by a heavy scarf. Her eyes peered over it, somewhat wild. The other sister: faint and faded, smudged. She came and went. She whispered. Her loafers had shiny pennies in them. Sprenger was the tallest of the family: with "talent." With "genius." He stank and did not shave his blondish fuzz. He was intransigently dull. He was ludicrous and embarrassing becoming friendly with the boys on the block.

The house was full of gadgets and the family. They shifted and moved in a restless surge. The mother wore her overcoat and hat and sat on the edge of a chair in the kitchen. The father picked his nose and drank coffee. Sisters came and went. One peered from the dark bathroom at Gibby, Kenny, and Donnie G, who sat on the couch, watching Sprenger set up the screen to show movies. They'd come for movies and they'd watch them, no getting out of it now. Sprenger was surprised too at finding his family home. This was a night for supper out and a double feature. Take the sister to a double feature.

She could giggle and eat Necco wafers, wrapped in her scarf in the dark.

Without his fucking family here, ole Spreng could've given his friends another terrific evening. But it had to be snowing, fuckin shit snow at Christmas! But it was pretty. Oh, the warm lights through the drifting snow! But his fuckin family had to stay in. Letem go out in the drifting snow! He could've hacked a number painting to pieces with his cavalry sword. Stuck his cock in a milk bottle. Lotsa laughs for good ole Gib an Ken an Don. Good guys! Showem a fuckin newsreel! Givem some beer! Givem some smokes! Shit! He made good money in the plastic factory. Pall Malls. Chesterfields. Smoke em up!

The snow kept coming down. Mrs. Sprenger poised on the edge of the chair. Kenny jumped when the sister rushed past him, looking away, at the wall, into the kitchen, for some tomato juice, a slice of Kraft American and a piece of pickled cauliflower. She rushed back into the dark bathroom with her things. The other sister came out of the bedroom and stood against the wall, watching her father. Sprenger was into his twentieth try at getting the screen to hang even.

Ya got too much silver on the goddam screen, his father says. Too much silver. Too much goddam glare. I tolja to let me mix the goddam paint up for ya. No, you know it all. You think it's a goddam radiator?

Choke, ya basted! Sprenger says. He is struggling with the screen. The three guests sit, their legs touching, squeezed together on the cluttered couch, trapped between great sliding piles of *Modern Romances, True Confessions, Police Gazette,* and *Silver Screen.* Some have slid to the floor but nobody has the courage to pick them up. The room stinks of Sprenger's feet and stale tobacco.

Boys, Sprenger's father says, woddaya think of a son who calls his father a basted an wishes him dead? HAH?! They jump and mutter, some more magazines slide to the floor. They don't think anything. They have no fathers to think anything about. Mrs. Sprenger is heard from the kitchen, Lissena ya father, boy, lissena ya father, boy. Twice. Her chair creaks.

Choke, ya basted slut, Sprenger says. He's got the screen up. It is dazzling silver, aluminum, nickel, chrome. The overhead light flashes and sparkles off its surface.

And now! For the first run! Extravaganza! Movie of the year! Sprenger goes to the projector and starts it, focuses the light on the screen, then shuts the projector off. He turns to his father. The lights, Dad? and his father turns them off. There is a rush of air into the room and the masked sister runs to the kitchen with an empty glass. She laughs and shuffles, scraping around on the linoleum. Juice, juice, she says. Pickle juice.

And now! Sprenger says again. On your sil-ver sca-reen, Spa-renger productions presents! Its Academy Award Special! The projector goes on and Sprenger sharpens the picture. Two little girls on a lawn. Sprenger's mother and father flank them, smiling and stupidly waving their arms. They make faces at the camera. One little girl dances ceremoniously from one foot to the other. The second little girl scuttles behind her mother and hides, and the father pulls at her arm to get her out in view again. A man in a white intern's suit enters the picture. White shoes. He smiles, clearly, and waves at the camera. Then he turns and speaks to the father and apparently the hidden child. The other daughter continues dancing.

Too much fuckin goddam silver.

Choke, you bottle-assed basted.

The young man in white faces the camera again and hooks his hands around his lapels, yanking at them, looking wise and kindly.

Hey, Dad! Dr. Gillespie! Remember he'd imitate Dr. Gillespie?

Too much *goddam* silver paint! Looka the goddam glare! Ya can't see anything!

Jesus *Christ!* Sprenger yells and then the film starts to speed up and skip, then goes black and white and black and white and stays white. A snapping sound is repeated regularly from the machine.

Sprenger crosses the room and turns the light on. Too much goddam silver paint, his father says, An now, ya got the goddam film in wrong.

Ah, fuck you *an* the film. Right, guys? He turns to the three guests, sweating and stiff on the couch. They laugh. Yeah, Donnie says . . . I mean—

Yeah. Fuck the film. Dr. Gillespie in a pig's ass! Sprenger wrenches at the reel and snaps out twenty or thirty feet of film, then opens the window. He lights a match and touches it to the bunched loops, then throws the flaming clump, reel and all, out into the storm.

Okay? he says to his father. Okay? We don't hafta see any more glary goddam movies! Okay?

Can't do a fuckin thing right, his father says. He turns to the boys. You boys want some coffee? Some tomato juice, maybe? From the kitchen they hear Sprenger's mother and the sister laughing. Juice, juice, pickle-ickle juice, they sing quietly and contentedly. A sound of shuffling feet, dancing.

SPRENGER
Happy New Year

SPRENGER'S GIRL broke off with him just before Christmas. He was crushed. What really depressed him was that he'd gone into debt to buy a whole new wardrobe to take her to the annual holiday dance at Our Lady of Perpetual Help. It wasn't the money spent that bothered him, but the distaste of seeing the clothes, in his mind's eye, getting filthy and greasy, without their ever having been worn for any sort of special occasion. He had been gone on this girl, although no one had ever seen her—he wouldn't take her to the neighborhood at all. Artie Salvo told everyone he had seen him on a bus downtown with some ugly Polack broad, but that of course could have been one of Sprenger's sisters.

Now, the big New Year's Eve party! "To forget," he said. Everybody would come, booze, food, laughs, music —even girls! His mother and father were going out, one sister was going to a party, the other was still in the nuthouse.

Gibby and Kenny stood on the corner outside Yodel's waiting for Carmine. They knew he wasn't coming. They waited for him because they didn't want to go to Sprenger's yet. They knew that they would finally go there, but not yet. Where is Carmine? Kenny said. He went to a decent party probly, Gibby said. Sprenger's is a stiff, right? Let's face it. No girls, no laughs, no nothin but booze. OK, where do you wanna go? Kenny said. Oh shit, let's go, Gibby said.

They saw the windows lit up and heard music coming from the apartment. He's home. Kenny laughed. What a break! He rang the bell and waited, then rang again. The buzzer sounded and they started up the stairs, at the top was Sprenger, a fedora on his head, his Civil War cavalry sword stuck in his belt, almost scraping the floor. O Christ, Kenny said, O Christ, Spreng, I didn't know it was a sword night—it's New Year's Eve for Jesus' sake. No no, Sprenger said, I was showin some stuff to my cousin Jules, he's in town an came over for the party, you know, get some stuff. Photographic stuff an the sword. What's the hat? Gibby asked. My old man's fedora, Sprenger said. He tilted the hat, sporty. Is that all—two of ya? Yeah, Gibby said. They went in. Nobody else here? They'll be here, Christ, it's only ten thirty.

The apartment was as usual, a gigantic garbage dump. Sprenger poured both of them a big drink of Kinsey. You got ice? Kenny said. It's gone, I'm makin some, my prickassed old man used it up on the sooper.

Jules came out of Sprenger's bedroom, picking his nose. He looked deformed, his eyes were big marbles behind incredibly thick lenses. No girls? he said. Let me take your coats, boys. No girls, Edgar? You told me a big party with girls to make you forget. They'll be here, Sprenger said. Maybe soon, Kenny said, everybody knows about ole Spreng's party! He seemed honestly enthusiastic as he drank his whiskey.

Hours later, three of them sat in Sprenger's room, all very drunk. Jules was dunking gingersnaps into his booze and the phonograph was turned up so loud that they sat numbed, Jules carefully depositing snots on the speckled walls, nodding, off time, to the band. Gibby lurched up. Kenny looked at him and Gibby shouted into the great blasts of brass and rhythm from the Herman band, Ice! Ice! I-C-E! Ice! Ice! Some! Ice! Kenny cupped a hand behind his ear and Gibby walked out of the room into more blasts of sound from the radio, some MC, crowds, horn tooting, laughing, from a hotel in midtown. Sprenger was in the kitchen, at the table, looking out the window. Snow was beginning now, the streets a white glow, the snow sifting under the streetlights in the bitter wind. Some people were leaving a bar across the street, blowing horns into the gale.

Ice, Gibby shouted. He went to the refrigerator and pulled out an ice tray. Frigid water spilled over his hand, but the water had frozen at the bottom of the tray, so he knocked the half-formed cubes onto the kitchen table, shoveled them into his glass, then filled it to the top with the rotten whiskey. Hey, Spreng! he shouted. Sprenger turned around, crying, then he started to wave a piece of paper at Gibby. She didn't hafta typewrite the fuckin letter! She typewrited the fuckin letter! She typewrited her fuckin *name!* Her *name!* Gibby swirled the ice around in his glass, Ah fuck it, he yelled. Have a drink, we got some ice now.

Shoes! An a suit! A fuckin new suit! A suit for the fuckin Cathlic dance! Fuck all the Cathlics! Amen, Gibby shouted. Looka these pants, he screamed, looka these blue pants. He had grabbed the pants by the creases and was shaking them back and forth on his bony legs. They look like shit, Gibby shouted, peering at them. They are shit, Sprenger yelled. The dance! he screamed. Oh, for Christ sake, let's turn off the fuckin radio, Gibby shouted. He walked over and turned it down, they could hear the phonograph now and the horn blasts from the street, tearing swiftly apart in the wind.

Fuck you, Sprenger yelled at the street. He pulled off his shoes. Fuck Flagg Brothers, he yelled. He threw the shoes through the windowpane. The snow blew in instantly in a big gust and the kitchen began to get cold almost immediately. Sprenger had his pants off then and threw them into the street. He picked up his cavalry sword and lunged at the paper he held in his other hand, skewering it, then rushed into the living room and plunged the sword into the couch. Gibby followed him, weaving, banging against the walls. Where are the fuckin broads! Sprenger yelled. The party! Jules came out of the bedroom. Are the girls here? he said. How many came? It's cold in here, Edgar. Kenny followed him out, leaned against the door jamb. Where's the ice, he said.

1946

SPRENGER
The Boulevardier

RIGHT AFTER the holidays, Sprenger disappeared. No one saw him anywhere, nor did he call anyone to come up and visit him, listen to records, watch his old newsreels, drink beer in his room. No one really missed him, but he had been a fixture, a kind of visiting apparition, for so long that his absence was duly noted. It never entered anyone's mind that he might have got himself a girl, for nobody in the neighborhood ever thought of Sprenger in those terms. Those stinking feet. The ripped canvas shoes, the shirts stained under the arms and down the front, the stubble of blondish beard on his chin. A girl was unthinkable.

The idea, in fact, wasn't even halfheartedly entertained. No girl, no matter what kind of pig, would go out with Sprenger. If his feet stank to the guys, what then would they smell like to a girl? An if his feet stink, wattabout his crotch, Artie Salvo said. It was a point.

But one Saturday evening about seven, he walked into Gallagher's. Gibby was at the bar with Carmine and Pat Glade when he walked in, smiling, his teeth a trifle less green than usual. His frayed blue melton overcoat was freshly cleaned and pressed and he wore a thirty-five-dollar Crawford suit, the two-pants variety. His shirt was so stiff with starch that the collar had dug a red crease into his throat just below that monstrous Adam's apple. Stiff, imitation silk tie, blue shadow stripe, the knot almost straight. The three of them stared at him. Even his shoes were shined! No one had ever seen Sprenger in shoes before, canvas oxfords with thick rubber soles were his speed—blackened and tattered, the heels worn down so that he walked bow-legged.

I don't believe this, Pat said. What the hell is this? Somebody musta died. Spreng, somebody die? We're sorry. Gibby nodded. Wotta tie that is, kid! That's what one calls elegance! Elegance! In the flesh. We heard *you* died, Spreng, Carmine said. Wottaya think, Patsy? Is he dead? Pat was drinking his beer with relish, and shook his head, the glass still to his mouth. He's gettin confirmed, he said. Soldier of Christ.

Sprenger, throughout this, looked at them with disdain. I'm going to a dance, gentlemen. A Coke, Martin, he said to the bartender. Is it funny to get dressed for a dance? You guys, of course, wouldn't know—hangin around the corner here. I've been doing a lot of thinking, about my life. He was serious. Gibby looked at him. What's your conclusion, Spreng? I see you bought a pair of shoes—that's *got* to mean something. The shoes are shined. You got a tie, as noted, right, Carminootch? An a Crawford Bond Street Executive Special suit, Carmine said. With extra pants for those casual weekends. This means, plus the fact that you're goin to a dance, the suspicion that you got a girl. Am I right? He pointed at

Sprenger, who was ordering a second Coke.

What's funny? Sprenger said. You don't come around no more, Pat said. You got a tie an a paira shoes an you quit us all. We've been thinking and wondering about you. I was having a discussion—in the library—with Cheech an Donato about you the other day. They—*we*— feel somehow—*betrayed.* Ah, Sprenger said. He sipped at his Coke. I've outgrown this, the corner, hangin around, the poolroom, Yodel's . . . I'm thinkin about the future, you gotta start thinkin about the future. You guys . . . I'm thinkin about a *home.*

It is a girl, Gibby said. What's her name, Spreng? Where she come from? God grant she's a Catholic girl, Pat said. An Irish Catholic girl. Ah, God grant it.

It's a girl, Sprenger said, a lotta things. Things to do, like I said, I can't be hangin around here all my life, fooling my life away, drinking beer. You drink Coke, Carmine pointed out. You know what I mean, Sprenger said. I've sort of—he was superior now, a trifle condescending—found myself. I got important things . . . to *do.* Not just stand around talking a lotta shit.

He looked out the window. Well. He gestured carelessly. I guess I'll grab a taxi and pick her up. He swirled the ice around in his glass, looking at the hack stand where Eddy Bromo was standing, leaning against his cab checking the results. No hard feelings, he said. You just, *one* just, grows up! His teeth flashed a light green and his Adam's apple bobbed as he lifted his glass to throw off the last of his Coke. He flung the glass carelessly against his mouth and the rim struck his chin, the glass tilting, Coke and ice cascading down chin and neck and onto his tie and shirt front, staining quickly, amber. He set his glass on the bar and wiped clumsily at the spreading stain with one hand, pulling his overcoat together with the other. They looked at him. Have a good time, Spreng, Gibby said. One tires of the old ways, Pat said. One does, Carmine agreed. You are a knockout, my boy! A knockout! Our greetings to the . . . little woman, Pat said.

BLACK TOM
Dead

THAT WINTER Tom died. They found him in the cellar, stretched out on his cot, in work shirt and stained pants, holding a black rosary in his hands. The county medical examiner did a postmortem on him and said that cause of death was malnutrition. He'd just starved himself to death, one day so weak he couldn't get up, and then he'd died.

The years since the war broke out in Europe were very bad ones for Tom—his family stuck in Ireland, U-boats and cannon between them. The English had done it, that Tom knew. They ruined the world with their manners and fake courage. The Germans took up arms against them, to rid the world of that mentality. So he brooded and starved, the letters from his wife late, in bunches, which he read over to himself after his potatoes.

He'd left some sock, everyone said, marvelous legend. All the poor, the infirm, crippled and retarded, were rich, Tom was no exception. Hundreds, thousands, sewn into his mattress, buried under the floor of the cellar, stuffed into rusted boxes and dusty jars and bottles.

They found enough cash to bury him, and started proceedings to send the balance to his wife. Put him into Holy Cross with a simple marker and a low requiem mass. Father Donovan, North of Ireland convert, said the mass.

Some thought it was plenty of money anyway, the depression persisting in their concept of dollar-value. But, thoroughly conscious of the bales of money being pumped out of the war economy, brought themselves up to the present, and realized that they could and would make more in six months—if the war went on. Not that any American boys should get killed. Only the heavies got killed, the Americans drilled through arm or shoulder got up, through the hospital with pretty nurses and cheesecakes of Betty Grable and Rita Hayworth, laughing, back to the lines, to get the lousy Krauts and Nips.

Father Donovan was a bit put out saying the low requiem, being next in line for the monsignorship. But this was a good man, "humble, devout, and hardworking" who regularly received. And then Father Donovan remembered him, thin and vaguely blue at the altar rail, smell of dry pungent sweat from his clothes as he raised his head, the coated tongue protruding. He had always made the priest a little sick. "Queasy" is the word he used when he thought of it.

1949

THE FIRE

THE ABSOLUTE REALITY of death, coming to the neighborhood. Not old people dying, somebody's grandfather, or distant cousin, old, in Chicago, anonymous coffin being carried down the steps of Our Lady of Angels. A young girl, dead at sixteen, a high school girl who knew all of the custard crowd, and had been going out with George

Berl regularly. To those not in the crowd, she was a little whore, yet they envied George. Now she was dead. He walked around for a month in a kind of envelope of silence, a pariah, locked into what they knew to be grief, as they had learned it, out of the movies. It was, indeed, a movie they had all seen over and over again, the same movie with different faces, here in the streets: real. Or the *Daily News* spreading to encompass them all, a living photo in the center fold. TRAGIC DEATH.

Burned to death in Staten Island in a swift brush fire, perhaps started by the Boy Scouts who helped the firemen fight the blaze for hours afterward. She had been ringed by the flames with George and the others who had gone on the picnic out to Latourette Park; the Dobbs brothers, Paul and Richie Camden, Cooky, Fink and his girl. At first they laughed, running away from the flames, and toward the small creek parallel to the road and the woods, and then they stopped laughing and ran, hard, the fire moved swiftly from behind them to each side and spread quickly, closing before them, till there was an open space just twenty feet wide in front, through which they escaped.

Except for Joan, who accidentally kicked off a loafer and when she had got it again and put it on, the fire had closed the gap and everyone else was outside it. She could hear, perhaps, their voices from the road, maybe even see them, the images shimmering, they called for her to stop fooling around. Johnny Dobbs was absolutely sober now, holding George's shoulder. They all knew that she was trapped, suddenly knew that; she was trapped and she was going to get burned. She was going to die. Joan Crawford, Barbara Stanwyck, this small-boned girl.

George ran toward the fire, trying to get through, to see her through the flames, but he was driven back, his hands and face burned, his eyebrows and hair singed.

116

He thought he saw her through the raging, collapsing brush but it might have been simply the blaze shifting. But he heard her, she was calling him in agony and terror, I'm burning. George, I'm burning.

She was buried out of Our Lady of Angels, the custard crowd and school friends, relatives, all in attendance. Death out of a movie, headline death, the center fold. And as those deaths, it was old a week later, though her friends were solemn beyond their need and desire. In that they lived, they were heroic. George Berl then, a month later, had moved in on Fink, and was dating his girl. But it had happened. Nobody remembered seeing her sister after that, in school or out. The family had perhaps moved, out of some sense of embarrassment, or guilt—to be alive: to shop: to wait for the bus: to study Spanish and Typing.

1950

BURLY
Floats Through the Air

IT WAS unutterably *de trop* when it happened. He thought that, but not the French phrase. Simply, some brief laugh, in the air, flying calmly, almost practiced, through the air down toward the cement cellar floor. He held very tightly to the half gallon of white port with one hand, the other clawed and groped, rather elegantly, in the air. His head was lower than the rest of his body. Ass over head. This phrase perhaps, he did think. He was aware it was a warm day. He was almost sober, just, somehow, had tripped over his own feet, or on a loose nail and was floating down. He held the white port tightly, lifted it up and out of the way of the banister. If he should land softly . . . not to have that good grape all over the floor, mixing with coal dust. He came down however, very quickly, it was almost, the gestures of arms and hands, abrupt, then he hit the cement very hard, right on his head, and broke it. The half-gallon jug broke a split-second later, as his arm came down, flat, and hard, dead weight. Death's weight. But that moment suspended was, in a sense, miraculous. All the possibilities thrown on his brain before him for the brightest flash then blinking out as the moment of floating collapsed into the downward, very rapid plunge, to his broken head. As his head broke (which he certainly "heard") his arm was still high in the air, the jug at the end of it, virginal. He did not hear that break, some small mercy. Sober, or for him sober. Too much. He floated. He laughed, briefly, his eyes straight before him on the coal pile on the cellar floor, arm above him in a gesture of ritual nobility, the other arm out, the hand in its small gestures of useless assistance. He floated.

1951

FADING OUT
Monte the Count

HIS OPEN IRISH FACE had become coarsened and brutalized, and he frequently, now, forgot his name, his real name. He always answered to "Monte" or "Count." A broken nose, reddened face with the ruptured capillaries speckling its surface. At times, through the alcoholic murk, the pain screwing his face up.

Let the pricks jus hit me one good shot on the toppa

the head. Jus one, jus one. He would cry at times, racked with sobbing, holding himself together, one hand on his belly and the other on top of his head, squeezing the life back into himself. (Beeoo Gesty! Beeoo Gesty! Cantering down toward Pep.)

Hermes Pavolites, one of three brothers who shot pool in Sal's, fair sticks, hit him a hard uppercut in the Melody Room one night, while Monte was looking at the bar in a daze, his head on his chest. Some bitter revenge taken at an opportune moment, for some old wrong done in the years just after the war. His two brothers stood near, in case Monte got up, but he simply sagged and oozed across the bar, spilling his beer and change into the rinse water. Everyone watched the Greeks walk out, laughing, then the place emptied.

Monte tried for months to find out who'd creamed him. Nobody had been there. Not me, Monte, I heard about the lousy fuckin thing, musta been some spicks come inna bar. To watch him walk the streets, asking questions, then finally stop, just look accusingly at everyone. One night he hit Frank Bull in Henry's, and Frank simply tore the arms off his shirt, laughing at him.

A little while later, the cops broke his arm outside Papa Joe's, one kneeling in the small of his back, holding his face down, pressed into the sidewalk, while the other casually whaled at his arms and legs with his nightstick. He broke Papa Joe's front window with the cast when he got out of Raymond Street jail.

DOLAN
Fading Out

BARGE THROUGH YEARS and get to that. Who to remember him? So many of them to be dead in foreign places, or bringing their deaths home, burning through them. Or simply, the cumulative effects of Americanism, eating at the soul, thence spreading throughout the whole organism in symptoms of alcoholism or other social despairs. But that was a particular day when he "faced the music." Or it faced him. He was literally its instrument. The Delphic Oracle, idiot girl straddling her tripod, swinging in the caldron, her foaming lips giving the truth. Really. Hers at least. Anyone could pick it up. Moved by song, their truth. Language.

So Dolan, florid of face, as in early Technicolor movies everyone had seen, the unhealthy blush of decay, turned the corner that day. The kids at their stickball game, elegant in their intensity. Dolan was going home to eat and fall asleep to the illegalities of "Mr. District Attorney." That he cared not a shit about. A "few with the boys" he would say, dozing. The decay settling comfortably in with really no cause left for it to be pinned on. A perfectly solid life, far back in the remote neighborhood of his youth, he felt it begin, then it became normalcy. Or it was normalcy the moment he took his position. Mr. Citizen. John Q. Taxpayer. Did his wife enrage him? Assuredly not. A simple contract, worked out and suffered with some style. That day as he rounded the corner, the children choreographed on the asphalt, a bright green broomstick a blur in the air. The song possessed him. An instrument of song.

He sang drunkenly in the sunlight, his eyes squinting in the glare. He sang to the children with great warmth and care, the lack of all professionalism in that he heard the whole song, and cared nothing for its separate parts, its weight of diverse elements. Such simple song. There he stood, the sunlight garish on that Hollywood flush. He sang, dying there before them in the sunlight, on that street in 1940. On his way home, clear within that most subtle pain of his whole presence.

1935

68th STREET
Introduction to the Boys

It is the boys on the street he must get through, meet them. The investigation. The interrogation. They wait for him in the shade across the street from his stoop, in the sun, in which he sits, glancing at them, pinching a new Spalding. They are casually arranged in front of Warren's apartment, openly staring at him. Further down the block, a few girls are sitting on another stoop, playing jacks, they do not count, they will be learned later, as encountered, beings to punch and thump. But the boys.

Must be got through. Who is he, this dark kid, a stranger, he looks at them starting a game of bottle-cap Banker Broker.

At four o'clock he crosses the street into the shade and watches the game. It will be another two hours before his mother comes home. What's your name, kid?

Angus says. Gibby, this kid says. Gibby? Angus laughs, then Artie Salvo, Bubbsy, Little Mickey, Warren. Gibby? What's yours? Gibby says to him. Angus, he says. Oh. A long silence, they all wait, Gibby squeezes the ball. Angus? Jeez, what a name. His smile is fixed, plaster, the face frozen.

So it will be Angus who will rise to fight him, a flurry, an awkward dance, they aim, in fashion, at each other's biceps with the knuckle of the middle finger protruding. Black-and-blue marks, tender and aching for days, the clear end sought. They break apart, both sniffling, the others are shifting to allow him to sit when Artie asks, does your mother *work?* The question asked, simply, for information, but Gibby hears it as insult, God, that helpless poverty, the missing father. Roaming through the streets from morning till night, waiting for her. Bewildered.

So Gibby shoves Artie, who gets up. The new fight, which no one wants to see, or be part of. That ends of itself, falling away, dissolving, the two of them openly crying, isolate, their arms hanging down and away from their skinny bodies, already stiffening, the others formally obstreperous, resuming the game.

1938

VISION OF DOOM
Big Mickey

CUTTING ACROSS the back yards to lose his pursuers in the Blackwell game, then over the fence into Warren's yard, and going down the stairs, Mickey tripped and fell and knocked himself out on the concrete. He came to a minute or two later, blood on his head, no sounds from the back yard, in front of him the ash-gray pants of Black Tom.

Tom put his hand out to help the boy up, and Mickey looked up at him. That hot day. He saw his own specific disaster in Tom's eyes, the fear of him for that man! A gaunt face, the eyes without luster, his faded shirt. His hand was out.

Mickey got to his knees and pushed past Tom, shoving him out of the way, the horribly gaunt face impassive, the hand still out. What it was that got to him he could not say. He ran out to the street and Bubbsy and Artie Salvo were in front of him and he dodged them, took off down the block. His own particular disaster of a life thick in his stomach as he ran, he turned and looked over his shoulder, expecting to see Black Tom pursuing, soundless. Horror. Bubbsy and Artie were loping after him, lazy in the hot sunshine. At the entrance to Warren's cellarway, at the top of the steps, Tom leaned against the metal fencing. All around him the heavy sunlight, the heat.

1947

COOKY
The Money

COOKY, with fur coat, gray Persian lamb, only the older women wore them, whose husbands had salted away that war-job money, to church on Sundays, walking afterward through the park, when the sun turned mellow in the spring. Sometimes they pushed, wore them into late May. Cooky had one. And nylons, high heels with ankle straps. Cordé bags, oversize, crammed with Pall Malls and Trojans for forgetful lovers. Hats, velvet or velour, with veils, and heavy, sloppy makeup. There she stood, or walked, wobbled on her heels.

Outside the frozen custard stand between Yodel's and Pat's Tavern, with the custard crowd. They hung around outside that stand, milling on the sidewalk, leaning against parked cars at the curb. Johnny and Roy Dobbs, Jimmy Lately, Berl, Doc, Paulie Camden sometimes, Fink. Their girls, that Irish-American look, vapid but smug, the lower middle-class leap to success. In sloppy-joe sweaters, plaid skirts, bobby sox and loafers or saddle shoes. The boys in pegged pants, heavy-soled shoes, sports shirts with upturned collars, buttoned to the neck.

Cooky in the middle of it, a slut, more than the others, or apparently so. Tough, without any age at all. With money. Plenty. Buy the crowd all the frozen custard they wanted, charlotte russe, jelly apples: or beer, whiskey, sweet wine for sex in the park. She went for Johnny Dobbs and Lately, they were the toughest. Or the crudest. The cruelest, certainly, with a fixed, ratlike cruelty, unswerving devotion to pain and harassment. Wobbling on her ankle-strap heels, her smile smeary upon them.

He would pop out of a Cadillac or Packard, at odd times; some man: it must have been, or it might as well have been, her father. The wide-brimmed pearl-gray hat, crease straight down the center of the crown, navy-blue melton overcoat, black double-breasted suit with a disappearing pinstripe, severe, black, French-toe shoes. He would smile and look at her, hand her bills, rolled up tight, or she would simply open the cordé bag and he would drop the money in. At any time, sometimes three or four days in a row, sometimes only on Saturdays or Sundays, or on week nights. When he saw her, and had money, he gave.

It was all right unless he did it in front of the crowd. Then she would lose control and hand the bills around to everyone, in front of him, she didn't care. Nor did he. It was an accident, if it happened, it happened, he certainly didn't go out of his way to avoid it. She gave the money out, determined, every bill, fives and tens, always those, maybe a hundred dollars or a little more or less. The custard crowd would whoop and dance around, the man would climb back into the car, where a friend or two waited, sartorial replicas vaguely, distantly smiling, uncracked. Cooky waited for something to happen, to go to somebody's house, to dance, to get drunk, go to the park with anybody, go any damn place, anywhere. The money got everything going fast, that would begin the day, or evening, right there.

One afternoon, bitter cold, after it had happened, the money given out, the crowd manic with varied possibilities, she stood, lighting a Pall Mall, watching the car move into traffic. The custard stand owner behind her tapping his ring against one of his machines, shaking his head. All of them absolutely—Nothing, he said aloud. These kids. These—people. All nothing. Crazy. Crazy. Nothing. Crazy.

The neighborhood thought of him as a kike with funny politics, ideas, maybe Red.

1944

BURLY
Keepin Outa Mischief Now

Burly was on the coal pile in the cellar underneath the ice-cream parlor. Hellberg's. His sister, Anna, worked there, behind the counter. Burly drank from the gallon jug of muscatel and then looked at it. Half gone, but he was drunk already. There was a smell of paregoric off him. A lot of people thought it was formaldehyde. This huge, sweating corpse.

Fred! Freddy! His sister was calling down the stairs to him. Did you get the hot-water heater fixed yet? Burly moved comfortably in the sliding coal. Fixin it, Anna, he croaked. Hurry up, the high school crowd'll be in soon an you know how we bla. Burly yelled something at the voice, which went on for a while. He heard the door close. Keepin outa mischief now, he sang. Keepin around the black and blue cow. Oh! La de da de da de de dee. He drank some more.

Fuckin Red, ho ha. Red was Phil Yodel. He was almost bald, so Burly called him Red, thinking to insult him. He wanted to call him Jewboy, but somehow liked him too much. It disturbed him to like Phil. The Jewboy. He drank some more muscatel, then reached into his coat pocket and took out a brown bottle of paregoric, uncapped it, and drank about a third of it. He chased it with more wine.

No formaldehyde for me! Keepin outa the great big chow! Yeah. I could strain it maybe, through bread. It's poison, he said to the broken heater. Knock you on your ass like a stiff. He sniffed under his coat but the sweetness of his breath overpowered his sense of smell.

Oh, the black and white cow, I wanta get some good chow, scramble two, down an draw one, Oh an how. He started flipping chunks of coal toward the foot of the pile, from his throne. Underneath him, buried about a foot down, was a full gallon of white port. The solder money. For Hellberg, the old Nazi bastard could afford a hundred fuckin hot-water heaters. Solder. Chewin gum an spit an a prayer. Keep me outa mis*cheef!*

126

He'd go down to Gallagher's and talk to Pepper, the goddam rummy. He sloshed the muscatel around in the jug and looked through it at the coal. Black-red, mysterious. It glowed inside and outside the jug. His fingers and lips were numb. Oh mischief, oh mischief, oh big big mischief, a now-ow. He buried the muscatel.

1948

DOLAN
The Heart, Pierced

AFTER MOPPING Yodel's floors and Pat's floors, and, if he was lucky, Gallagher's floors in the mornings, he'd take his few bucks and get his wine, and get out of it in the park, or in a doorway. And sing, the old songs, stiff, his head back in an incredible tension, his arms out stiff from his body, eyes closed, the listeners transfixed at the sweetness of the Irish tenor, so high and clear, strong and edged, cutting through the air all down the block, up, over the tops of the roofs, people coming out of Yodel's as if they had never heard such melody.

> Casey would waltz with
> The strawberry blonde
> While the band played on
>
> He'd waltz round the floor
> With the girl he adored
> While the band played on

he would sing. And "Mother Machree," and "One Alone." Chestnuts. The stink of sweat and piss. The stink of muscatel. Dolan, the voice, the angelic tenor, blind, reaching out to some lost tradition of song. I could back him with wire brushes on that, Al would say. Dolan! Encore! He would stand, his eyes closed, reeling then, into a doorway, the noise, normal, of the street, resuming, the heart of each pierced, each listener transfixed. The smell of piss and muscatel. The imagined applause of some music hall no one had ever seen, fine mist over the Liffey, the smudged streets of Dublin. Dolan, in the doorway, his fly open, his eyes closed, his arms stretched out on either side, going down into the muscatel awaiting him, the song lost in it.

His heart, transfixed. His heart, pierced. Bittersweet.

1949

THE MISUNDERSTANDING

MEYER DAVIS! Al said. Jesus Ke-rist. Meyer *Davis!* Lester Lanin, there's another sweet-as-peaches band. Da-de-da-de-da. Oh, Lester! Lanin! Lanin, Davis, and you got Blue Barron, not so exclusive or—ayleet, but a *swell* band, a really *swell* band with good arrangements. Vincent Lopez! He did a quick two-step into a Peabody and glided down along the counter to the paper stand. Guy Lombardo, another perennial favorite. You *have* to know how to *read* with those orchestras. Read the marks, read *all* the notes, little specky-weckies, bam! His hand shot out, ba-bam! ba-bam-bam-bam-bap-bam! *Paradiddle!* Bam! Rim shot, and ... into ... "Louise." Oh, they know how to play it just soft and sweet as a little kitten. That's my kinda playing. *Reading,* gotta read the little specks, the little bird shits on the sheets, and play every one *right.* "Canadian Capers." "Louise." "Dardanella," oh *sweet* Dardanella! And get the time right—4/4, 3/4, any time at all. The big boys want the drummer

to just sit right down on a date and play the whole reper-
twah, right off.

All the while Pepper was looking at him, starting to
feel the hangover very clearly and exactly now: in various places. The head aching from nape of neck to crown,
then down over the eyes and in them. The stomach flut-
tering and queasy. A rod of dull, hot iron from the throat
to the guts. Gas pains. Heartburn. He looked at Al, listening. Lousy drummer, lousy drummer, he said, getting up
from his stool and half-finished seltzer. Then he yelled:
You're a lousy! Rotten! Bum! Drummer! Al looked at
him, amused, but also annoyed. He was hearing those
bouncy, rippling arrangements in his head, the thin sug-
ary melodies, reedy vibratos. And you, dear Pepper, you,
are a drunkard. Not, not just somebody who likes a little
drop, but a drunkard, worse than Dolan and Burly put
together.

Pepper, grinning evilly through his brown-stained
teeth, his hand fishing for a handkerchief, to wrap it
then around the knuckles of his right hand. His face was
red. Dolan. Burly. They were *drunks.* They were *bums.*
I'm a fuckin banana checker, he said. A goddam good
banana checker, you bum drummer. You fairy drummer
with your nigger jazz. What are you? What *are* you? Can
you check in bananas? Thousands, *millions* a day? Hah?
You bum on unemployment. You faker, cheap faker
basted. What happened to Penny, hah? I'm gonna knock
you on your ass.

Al backed out of the store, wrapping his own handkerchief around his knuckles, then taking his glasses off
and placing them in his breast pocket. Phil said, Fellas,
take it easy. It's all in fun, a little argument. You don't
wanna hurt each other. Al stood in the street, looking up
and down, squinting to see, his eyes slits. A banana
checker! he suddenly screamed. You are a lepidoptera,
Eddy would say. A beetle! A glowworm! He saw Pepper's

dark shape in the doorway and started down Fourth Avenue toward the park. A banana-checking whiskey drunk! A beetle! A drain on the necessities of the nation! Pepper followed him. You nigger music player. No job, either, just like a nigger. Live in a goddam hotel with niggers in it too, I bet.

They disappeared around the corner of the next block, Al walking backward, Pepper pursuing, about twenty feet apart. Phil stood at the door, watching the white handkerchiefs gleam in the air. In about forty-five minutes they passed the store, having circled the block, Al still walking backward, Pepper after him, both of them furiously tugging at their handkerchiefs, adjusting them, rewrapping them. Al was screaming with laughter, every minute or so yelling Bananas, bananas! Pepper would reply Nigger bum, nigger bum! They retraced their original route.

They went around and around about a half-dozen times. The last time it was almost dark and when Pepper got to his corner he shook his fist at Al and walked toward home, unwrapping his handkerchief. Al stopped his back-pedaling and walked briskly to Yodel's, then into the store, his handkerchief still around his hand, his glasses on once again. Phil looked at him. OK, Al? Everything OK? But of course, dear Philip. Bananas! A banana checker telling *me* about the art of music, the art of drumming! I used to have a dog act, Philip! A *dog act!* In vaudeville. But this you know well, Philip. And now, a Coke! Pepper Banana! Trying to intimidate a man who has actually *given up* a show business career. Ke-rist Jesus!

FRIENDS
The Colloquy

AL HAD BEEN DISCHARGED from the Kings County psychiatric observation ward just that morning, and had spent the day in a kind of daze. He said nothing of the hospital, and looked sallow, shrunken, his face stubbly-bearded, clothes unpressed.

Now he was with Eddy, neither of them drinking men, they seemed a bit uncomfortable at Carroll's bar, in a hubbub of beer lushes and jukebox noise. They were both slightly drunk. It was late, and Al wanted Eddy to go home with him to see a new Zildjian cymbal he had got "on a trial basis" just before his incarceration in Kings County. Eddy doubted the existence of such a cymbal, and besides, he did not wish to accompany Al to his dwelling. He was tired, had a slight headache, music was assuredly, definitely, dear friend of my ripe years, not the thing for him at this late hour. But a cab! Al said, Right down to the house, my little room! Edward! A cab, a hop skip and jump and we're there . . . I just want to *show* you the cymbal! Ke-rist! You don't think I'd play drums at three o'clock in the morning? Your penchants are well-known to me, Mr. Pearson, Eddy said. Let me think it over, in the meanwhile, I shall have another glass of Seagram's whiskey and another glass of Ballantine beer.

Fifteen minutes later they were in the street. Al: one foot on the curb, the other in the gutter, his head swiveling from the street, looking, peering up and down for sight of a cab, then to Eddy, his hand on Eddy's coat sleeve. Eddy: leaning back against Al's weight, both feet planted on the sidewalk, picking his teeth with a matchbook.

Drumming, he said, drumming, you know, dear Mr. Pearson, is the bane of your existence—the henbane, I might add, expatiate upon, a deadly poison, deadlier than the well-known nightshade, which is one of the deadliest of all, without a doubt . . . what else was it that put you in the asylum, that house of utter remorse, but that accursed drumming? A cab, Edward, a cab for Jesus' sake, and it wasn't drumming, it was the fucking bureaucratic state, didn't want to give me my money, my unemployment money. Drumming, drumming has put you in the frame of mind where you are a sucker, I might say, a sucker for just such gilt-edged frame-ups. Music in general, one might add, has deceived you, the pounding of those drums! That Zildjian, Eddy baby, that Zildjian! Ka-changgg, ka-chazzz, chaz, chaz, chaz, chaz, ch-ch-ch-ch-chazzz, chaz! He had let go of Eddy's arm to flail away at the Zildjian. Music, as part of the quadrivium, fine, Eddy said, an excellent adjunct . . . my own banjo-playing as part and parcel of my entire, what shall I say, educational—*spot!* Fine, all well and good, but as some sort of nostrum! . . . Some what, Eddy, some *what?* What's that! What? Nostrum, is to think it something it is not, some panacea, which it is not. Nostrum, Al crooned. My own philological studies have furthermore convinced me that I myself have taken myself as a philologist, an entomologist, perhaps a trifle too seriously. All work and few adjuncts to one's overwhelming desire to get out of the basement makes Eddy a dull boy. Eddy, I got you, I got you, but this once. We'll have breakfast with a neighbor you must meet, a man of show business, the world of entertainment, oh, from long years ago, the Palace and places like that. A seal act,

Eddy! A seal act, do you get that, Jesus, Jesus, Ka-ka-ka-chazzzz! Women, though, said Eddy. Women, *there* is a nostrum for all ills. To speak quietly with one, to discuss books, the fruits of one's research with a charming woman, to have an *apéritif* in a charming café, in a charming city where one can be true and free to one's self, not this depaucitated—burg! To hold her—to FUCK her to a frazzle, a mere slip of a thing. That's it, Eddy. You gotta hear this seal-man, he's got stories about backstage at the Palace you'll die over. Ke-RIST, here! Right here in the USA, in little old New York town, not Paris, France. Make your mouth water, Eddy, make it just run over with water! Too much music is in your life, Doctor, you are a man of one-track enormities, a capable enough fellow, but, after all, did *I* go away to the insane asylum to have my cerebrum prodded? No. Did I smoke loosies on the floor of the lavatory watching old morons play with their pee-pees? Assuredly not. A branching out! The banjo, education, WOMEN, many things to assist one in avoiding the henbane of jazzy notes and rhythmic fiddling. *Jeu de mots!* Al shouted. A cab turned the corner, going away from them, started rolling downtown. Al whistled, but the cab kept going. You son of a bitch! Al yelled, A watcher of the feetball madness! Your manner, Eddy said, Doctor. Your manner was exceptional to even such a one of the ilk of cabdrivers, who might as well be driving around lumps of shit fashioned like jitneys. They *are* lumps of shit by all means at any rate. Come, Eddy, come, come and have some coffee at the Royal anyway, and we'll talk it over, be with me tonight, look at my Zildjian, talk with the seal-man! The *Royal?* The Royal Restaurant? A den of thieves and coleoptera, ragamuffins—at this hour filled with the lowest rabble of the streets! The Royal, Doctor? Eddy Bromo may be there with other comrades of the Shitrolettes, and the Shitmouths, and the Shitfords. Mechanics in the basement of life. All these years, I, who have been a *master* mechanic of the Cadillac motor car, a skilled worker of Rolls-Royces, to associate with such lowlife. I am penurious, but content, Doctor, I shall neither accompany you to your dwelling, nor to the Royal beehive, the cockaroach nest! Al released his arm, suddenly, and walked toward Senator Street, stood at the corner a moment, waving madly at him, then disappeared. Christ, he shouted, Ke-RIST! Eddy stood at the curb, looking at the corner where Al had just been. A cab was coming from the other direction and it slowed as the driver saw Eddy standing there. Begone, he said, waving it on, Begone, henbane of creatures, Henry Ford's turd! He stood a moment longer, lit a cigar, then started walking toward home. A charming woman, he said. A *French* woman. An *apéritif.* On the roof . . . on the *observation* tower!

1947

PEPPER
In the Sun

PEPPER WAS a binge drunk and prepared for those times when he would be tempted to oblivion by his family, a well-meaning but shrill group of women, shocked into a realization of their value as citizens by the money brought into the house by the war. He would prepare, getting the price on Paul Jones or Kinsey White Label quarts on the docks where he worked as a banana checker. He made a lot of money with his card but whiskey was whiskey. He had, indeed, a passion for the raw sweetness of cheap blends. He'd take the bottles home one or two at a time and stash them in a suitcase, when it was full he was ready. The rest of the whiskey he left in his locker on the pier. When the time came, he'd pick up his suitcase, grunting with the load of quarts, walk past the women, and get a cab to some downtown flea-bag.

This day, he was coming home, in very bad shape, shaking and white. The suitcase seemed as heavy as the night he'd left, though it was empty. Small crabs had been walking all over his blankets during the night, green and luminous, all over him, under the covers and sheet, around the room, up the lamp and walls. When he turned the lights on, they seemed bigger and he drank half of his last quart. Then they went away.

The sun was terrible on his head and in his eyes, standing in front of the Cities Service station across from Yodel's. He got out of the cab there so he could walk home, his suitcase swinging, into the house. A cold shower. A long afternoon sleep into the night and then all the next day. Eat some of Agnes' eggs even. He gagged and staggered. The sun was burning into his blue suit, his beard prickled and the sweat ran out from under his hatband.

He heard loud shouting and laughter. Johnny Dobbs and Frank Bull were outside Yodel's door, yelling at him, waving their arms and throwing down imaginary glasses of whiskey. In the shade. In the beautiful shade. He looked down toward his corner, the street viciously bright in the sun, the pavement white and glittering.

Whaddaya got in the suitcase, Pepper? That was Dobbs. It convulsed him and Frank.

Whaddaya got there, Pepper? That was Frank. Johnny slapped him on the back and they reeled around laughing. Frank poked his head in the door to say something to Phil, and Johnny hopped from one foot to another. Fat George came out and looked across at him, grinning. He too drank, long, from an invisible tumbler. Pepper couldn't move now: neither through the sun and home nor over to the shade and his audience. He felt his legs going and he tried to straighten up, then half-knelt on one knee on the suitcase, but it fell and he pitched forward, lying over it, looking at his hands protruding from his soiled cuffs. Burning, they were burning on the pavement. Out of the corner of his eye he could see hundreds of tiny crabs running toward him from the gas station. They were dazzling in their brightness.

1948

THE RAPE
The Meeting

PASTOR JOHNSON smiled at Al, entering the inner doors of the church, into a kind of subdued and genteelly hysterical din of organ music and singing. The White Robed Choir was starting in on "Rock of Ages," and at least half the congregation had joined in, standing and swaying to the heavy, unsophisticated chords Penny was getting out of the scuffed organ. Al smiled back, his hat in his hand, his Bible prominent, and moved his lips, silently saying, Pastor, to the man in black, standing on a small stage at the front of the church. Penny looked up and saw Al, smiled, a twisted thing, she hunched and twisted to the melody, her breasts moving under the white robe. In their drab and pimpled faces the White Robe Choir, lined up, their mouths open: they stood, catatonic. The congregation was almost all up now, yelling out the words, Pastor Johnson cutting the air in front of him to shreds with his hand, grinning and sweating. Al slipped toward the last pew and got into it, swayed along with the whole thing, the perspiring and delicately controlled throng. Rock of Ages! Sing any damn song! Her breasts under the Robe! Cleft for Me! She squinted at Al, she knew his position by the glitter of light off his glasses, his brilliant tooth. She whaled away at the organ, her hips rocking, her thighs sliding a little on the smooth old bench. Al could see her feet under the hem of the robe. That was new, tonight. High heels. Everybody in on it now, even old Johnson, who'd forgotten the words years ago, Rock of Ages, Rock of Ages, Rock of Ages! The congregation had taken on a glazed look, Penny going into another chorus, she could feel her own womanhood in the sense she had there of her warm flesh, thighs against each other. She spread them a little, so that her ankles bent inward, her heels aslant. Al was grinning, glittering from his whole face, sailing along on the old hymn, any old goddam hymn, you big-titted Honey! Then it was over, the congregation settled down into gibbers and moans, as they began wiping their faces Pastor Johnson sent them to hell with the beginning of a shrieking sermon. Oh Jesus! Oh Jesus! An old woman fell on the floor and writhed after a time, and an old man joined her, then a young woman worked her way out of the White Robed Choir and settled herself down, weeping, Al's eyes piercing in at her, watching her skirt slip up as she rolled carefully on the floor, her hands over her eyes. It went on, Penny was flushed, watching the rollers, wanting to join them, but join them—in some strange way? In what way? She flushed, she saw herself among them naked, Al watching her, touching her with understanding and pity. She began to cry and then gasp Jesuss, Jesuss, Jesuss, Jesuss, O Jesuss. Al threw his arms in the air and yelled, Oh, saved, saved! JEE-suss KE-rist!

Later, their now customary ice-cream soda in Hellberg's was strangely unsatisfying to Penny. She looked at Al over the porcelain-topped table, he was so *mature,* but she needed something of him, she needed to be with him longer, the ice-cream soda would end and then they'd part. They finished and walked out, the night sultry. May I walk you home, Penny? I know it's forward of me, but I feel that I know you so well, if I may I'd be so delighted, so—charmed! But if I overstep the bounds of, well . . . Please, Al, Oh, please do, I'd be so pleased, it would be an honor. Thank you, Penny. Al took off his hat.

In her hallway, he slipped his onyx pinky ring off, covertly, then, just as she thought he was going, he took her left hand, expertly fumbling, and slipped it on the ring finger. She looked at it, red and hot suddenly, then her eyes met his, Al, she said, oh Al. Sweets to the sweet, Al said, for you, Penny, as a merest token of my esteem and friendship, a trifle for the sweet in the name of Jesus, Our Saviour. Oh Al, oh Al. Al took off his hat and swept an arm around her, then held her close and kissed her on the mouth. She felt stunned, insane within her body that instantly began a raging and throbbing. He broke his lips away from her, still embracing her closely, and looked into her eyes, quietly and deeply said, I love you, Penny. She looked down, her eyelids fluttered, she looked up at him, into his bright eyes, and grinned, shy and smeary. She could feel his hot erection against her belly. Unbelievable, unbearable.

THE GREAT PITCH

YOU NEED this great pitch, Al said, to sell anything.
Greeting cards are absolutely no exception. Am I right,
Philip? Absolutely, Phil said. Gus leaned against the
soda cooler. Give us your pitch, Al. Let's say I'm the
customer, maybe I wanna buy some greetin cards an
maybe not. Ah, fiddlesticks! Al said, bullshit! *One* customer's resistance is nothing. I need armies, great
groups. In the subways is where I'll make the great
mark, tomorrow, it's possible for a man to make fifty,
sixty, even a hundred dollars a day in the subway, a
couple of hours could do it.

Suddenly he's in a car, swaying, hanging onto a pole
in the middle, his bag of samples down between his
ankles. He reaches in and pulls out two boxes of cards
—one "sentimental" and one "cute," opens both and
tucks the covers underneath so that the boxes rest in
them, propped up at an angle. I hold out my boxes, he
says, then walk slowly down the car till I get to some
kind old lady who's not reading the Daily Horseshit and
I thrust the sentimental box into her lap, Take a look at
these lady, twenty-five cards, a card for all occasions,
for what, not five, not three, not even a buck and a half
but exactly one dollar, everyone will love you, occasional cards on those days that everyone else forgets.
She's looking at the box, she tries to give it back to me,
but, you understand, gentlemen, I won't *accept* it,
rather, I whirl, dancing paradiddles down the car and
proffer the cute box to some little sweet cunt of a high
school girl, preferably with her boyfriend, so that he has

to take her books so she can see the box, take the box, he's delighted, it's another step forward in his quest to get into her panties—meanwhile the old broad is upset, she wants to give the sentimental shit back to me but I act as if I've forgotten all about it, I'm talking to this little high school broad and winking at her boyfriend, cute cards, little bunnies, little rabbits and bunnies, and puppies and kitties—any shit that comes to mind I conjure it up, I debate with them, I expatiate, they're looking at the cards, the little cunt is smiling—I'm getting a hardon thinking of her little ass—I whirl, paradiddle again, bam, rim shot, toward the old lady, whose neighbor is looking at the cards, look at them, I say—man or woman it matters not to me—look at them—do you think a man of my age and experience would be demeaning—only I say *lowering* to these proletariats—lowering himself peddling, *hawking* greeting cards in the subway if I didn't have something sure-fire, something that is such a bargain that the little item must go, must be sold, selling as a matter of fact, itself. Madame, I say, madame, figure it, twenty-five cards for one dollar comes to four cents a card . . . other people have been listening, I address the car, turn to look at my little cunty-wunty, now, you know, all of you—as consumers, they like that, to find out they're consumers, they always thought they were slobs—you pay at least a nickel for any card in the five-and-ten, and you know what a nickel card is like, it looks like a *nickel card*—any decent card must cost you at least fifteen cents . . . so here you've got twenty-five cards all of at least the fifteen-cent variety. Some look to me, although I don't buy cards any more, I have so many of these beauties, like quarter cards. I remove the box from the old bitch's hands, gently but forcefully, she wants the cards now, she's looking in her purse, the cunty's boyfriend comes up with his moolah, there's a rush, I have to run to my big suitcase to fill the orders before the train comes to the station, twenty boxes, that's ten bucks for Al . . . I'll have an assistant working for a buck an hour carrying cartons on a hand truck, following my route, restocking me when the supply runs out. Maybe a banner or something on the suitcase, Pearson's Follies, red and white, or with blue and stars, there's no limit, anything goes with mighty Al. Later, a station wagon, gold, filled with boxes of cards, cuties, sentimenties, any fucking cardie your heart may desire, religious cards—he whipped his hat off and back on in one motion—any fucking thing, pictures of fucking bleeding Jesus, the Pope, Rita Hayworth sucking a nigger's cock, anything, big gold station wagon, I'll have a PA system, and a Plexiglas plastic dome on the goddam thing, stand up there in a red tuxedo, AL PEARSON'S CARD SERVICE, one buck, a card for all occasions. I'll have to beat them off. In a year, maybe two, I'll work the whole shebang out of the heliport, deliver all over the city, the state, and—to ships at sea! Jesus Ke-RIST, Philip! His eyes were tearing behind his glasses. What if nobody wants your cards tomorrow, Al? Gus said. Suppose they say, hey, go fuck yaself. What about that? Then I'll follow the rules for atomic attack, Al said, as outlined in the Defense Manual. Lay down on the sidewalk away from all windows and shit in my hat.

1949

COOKY
The Main Attraction

SHE HAD COME BACK to tell everyone that she worked in a carnival, a road show, moving from city to city, up

there with all the old-timers—how *they* had started. Al
was amazed. Were there any dog acts? Any kind of animal acts at all? How about the girls? Red-hot mamas?
His eyes looked through Cooky's purple velvet dress,
bored into her underwear, down to the flesh—his tongue
darted around his lips. His glasses glinted. Oh for Christ
sake, Al, she said. You never got enough nookie, didja?
Worse now, it looks like.

Her old beaux were not around. Roy Dobbs was at sea
and Jimmy Lately—somewhere. She hadn't come to see
them anyway. Just the old corner on her way through to
Boston—suburb of Boston. The main attraction.

They would put her in a cake of ice, an enormous
block of ice, dressed in a G-string and bra, black net
stockings, heels—into the block of ice she went, eyes
closed. At the end of the show she'd come out, wet, smiling. The suckers gaped, clapped, went home and talked
about it for days.

She dressed almost as badly as always, garish, too
much makeup clumsily applied, short skirts, heels she
tottered in. Gigantic handbag slung from her shoulder.
She leaned against the soda cooler and chatted with Phil
and Al and everybody else who came in. Frank Bull
passed by, saw her, and came in to grab her ass. Hear ya
been in Hollywood, Cooky. Gotta eat the bird ta get up
high out there, right? Get any parts? She looked at him.
You still look like a fuckin ape ta me, Frank. You still
talk like one too. Like an ape, Al said. Doctor Beshary
will be delighted to hear—Go fuck you! Frank said, you
an that fuckin Joo basted, Eddy! Hollywood, shit, Cooky
said. I'm in show bizness, no goddam movies fa me.

Is the ice really ice, Cooky? Al said. Is it cold?

She stood against the cooler. She was the main attraction. Cookie LaNord. Frozen solid into a cake of ice.
She wanted to see everybody, all the old faces. Al was
looking at her legs and she leaned back further so that

her skirt hiked itself up a bit more. Ya coulda been a
great stripper, Cooky, Phil said. A fuckin tramp, Frank
said. He'd never been able to lay her. There he was.
Cooky looked over at him. Gettin more than you are,
Bull, she said. The fuckin ice-lady, shit! I'd rather have
Ruthie than you, any day. Good, Frank, good. I'll tell
Ruthie how ya feel about her . . . you look like a goddam
husband anyway—a potbelly an a halfa hardon.

1950

AL PEARSON
Drumming

AL WAS DRUMMING AT Yodel's counter. Rat-a-tatta, tat tat.
Paradiddles, Philip, paradiddles, he said. Gold tooth
glinting, his hands flashing as he drummed from the
marble counter to the lemon-lime syrup dispenser, over
to the Canada Dry dispenser. Rim shot now! and back to
the quick roll, snap roll, ahhhh, Philip, good as a juddy,
good as a *jeu de mots* any time. A—*musical*—juddy! You
ever hear those good society bands playing something
crisp, really sharp and perfect, Lester Lanin, for exam-
ple? "Canadian Capers?" Vincent Lopez? Ohhh, Philip!
Good enough to eat! He drummed on, harder now, getting into it, sitting now at a stool, hunched into his coat,
the sticks blurred as he drummed against his humming
of "Canadian Capers." Beshary and Fat Phil looked at
him. You should get a job, Al, Fat Phil said. You can play
over at the Hudson, right, Phil? Phil take ya over ta the
Hudson, right, Phil? You got an in there, ya must have,
ya been goin over there fa ten years ta jerk off every
week. Twelve years, Phil said. He looked up from the

Journal-American sports page. Ah, Al, you have the true touch, Eddy said. He walked over, took a matchbook out of his pocket and started to strum his knuckles with it.

Pepper walked in to buy some cigarettes. His toothless mouth sagged when he saw Al. Oh Jesus Christ. Chesterfields, Phil. Jesus Christ! He walked out. Pepper don't like your drummin Al, Fat Phil said. Pepper may burn his throat with himself, Al said, turning to Eddy, then Phil. Well, gentleman, do I get rated? On that one? Let's call it a bonny Al, whattayasay, Eddy? Al looked disappointed. Just a bonny? Eddy? Philip is correct Al, Eddy said. He was strumming furiously, bent over Al's shoulder. A *bon mot* for the Pepper repartee. A bonny it is then, Al said. Al never argues with the chiefs of the wit circle, right, Philip?

Fat Phil walked out and stood on the corner to watch the girls from the high school pass by. He shouted in at Al, Hey Al, you should getta loada some a these broads. Fuck "Canadian Capers" and Lester Lane. Al stopped drumming immediately and jammed the sticks into the pocket of his raincoat, then dashed out the door in time to see a little blonde pass by, about sixteen, small-breasted and with slender legs, swaying, her eyes straight ahead. Al whipped his hat off and swept it to the ground, falling to one knee, his tongue darting between his lips, smiling ferociously. Phil-lip! Phil-lip! he screeched. He bounded up and dashed back into the store. Suck her dry, Philip, suck her dry! Oh Christ, could I use her as an accompanist—on the old *skin flute!* Skin flute, Philip? Skin flute? Nothin for that, Al. That's old. He was at the window craning to see the little blonde. Eddy looked up from his *Green Sheet,* Ah, my ex-wife was more pulchritudinous, actually! Unfortunately, her brains were in her matrix. Her mattress? Al said. No, her matrix, Eddy said, but mattress—Oh, mat-

144

rix, Al said, and I said mattress. Aha, Eddy said. A—they looked at each other, Eddy shaking the *Green Sheet* over his head—*jeu d'esprit!* they both shouted, laughing, Al hauling out his sticks and pounding on the gumball machine.

1943

DONALD DUCK
Quack Quack

DUCK THE AVENGER. Duck the Righteous. Duck the Cruel. They'd quack him into the ground, to death. It began as soon as they found out that he objected to the old, honored name. He made the mistake of using his muscles on them. He had become absolutely mad about it, and reacted with a venom that at first surprised, then made them equally venomous.

He stood in the street, his arms apelike, swinging from his body. Bloody, pimpled face reddish-glowing in the light. Kill! Kill! He'd shout that. Crush! Kill! Crush! The gang would stand across the street from him in a loose, milling crowd, ready to break, begging him to charge them.

Quack! Quack! Hey Duck, hey, Ducky! Ducky, Wucky, hey! Quack! Quack! Duck. Quack. Kill! he yelled. Crush, throttle! Choke!

Some poor bastard would always be caught and choked and shoved to the ground until he promised he'd never, never, say Duck again. Or yell Quack. Or in any way suggest that this had been the Avenger's name for years and years. As soon as he got up—Quack! Quack! you son of a bitch! And Duck would chase him again,

Kill, kill, kill! Ah, that ravaged complexion.

He started going out with Dolores. To the movies, and walks in the park. She called him Don, of course, and had no way of refusing his attentions. He had punched and tormented her for years of childhood and this changed subtly and naturally into dating. When he kissed her at the door she closed her eyes to avoid seeing the acne. He'd cream his face, powder it, wash it to rawness with special soaps, coat it with ointments and greasy salves. Duck the Lover.

This emergence of sexuality spurred the rest on. Duck spent all of his afternoons after school plotting revenge and chasing his friends, at times getting into real fights with them when he would, out of his despair, handle them much too roughly. Then there would be bloody lips and noses, black eyes and terrible days of cold hatred and anxiety.

Until it would slowly slide back into the ritual of baiting, the shouting, ending with the christening of Dolores, Daisy. Quack! Quack! Raucous, leaping in the twilight, each staring at the outline her brassiere made under her blouse. That bastard Duck.

1940

DONALD DUCK
The Trolley Car Notebook

A SMALL, blue-marbled book, bound with a metal spiral at the top. In it, Duck, the pimpled, the slouching, the boy who flushed and swore when he was accused of masturbating, kept the numbers of the Fifth Avenue trolleys, Third Avenue trolleys, and 69th Street trolleys.

This was religious, a fetish and talisman to hold to. If his acne oozed, he had his book. A surety. He would sit at the kitchen table, eating his glassful of graham crackers and milk, and pore over the lists of scrawled figures. Gaps in every line, those missing trolleys that he had never seen, watching for months. They had to be there, motormen on them, the passengers facing each other on the wooden benches. But they were missing. Holes, spaces, filled with horizontal lines and asterisks for these lacunae.

He had seen now, for three weeks, the same street-cars each day. He knew the flaking figures on their red steel sides with an absolute intimacy. Top of the 2 broken; bottom of the 7 scarred; a 9 faded . . .

Fredo on the back of a 69th Street car one day, as Duck came around the corner. It was picking up speed and the street was crowded with trucks so that he couldn't chase it: a missing number, he knew it, one he had looked for for months, Fredo's tattered corduroys over the last three digits, he turning, seeing Duck, frozen, on the corner, his notebook in his hand, open, then waving, giving him the nonchalant stiff middle finger Fuck You Duck! and borne away toward Fort Hamilton Parkway.

1942

ARTIE SALVO
Born Ballplayer

TURNING AT SECOND BASE, Artie slipped on a grease slick and fell on his hip. That was the end of his ballplaying. He finished the game and limped home. The next day he couldn't get out of bed. Something with the bones. His hip wasn't exactly broken, it grated or rubbed or something, so after a while in the hospital he was home, walking with a cane.

In the movies one Saturday some kids knocked him down in the aisle, so that he fell on his hip again. This time he couldn't even get up and the manager took him home in a taxi. He went to the hospital again, and stayed for a long time, then was out on crutches. He'd watch the other guys play stickball. Bubbsy, Gibby, Angus, Warren—learned reactions. Stumbling around. Copying stances and gestures from baseball photos in the *News.* He felt his own muscles moving after a ball, a low, hard liner—effortless.

It could have been any of those other goddam saps— they could grow up to drink and eat and fuck gimpy. He was finished. He'd yell and clap, propping himself up on the crutches, balancing easily on the good leg, the other bent at the knee and swinging slightly, the shoe scuffing the pavement.

Tell them stories. The nurse with the big tits who'd press them against you when she gave you a rubdown. The fairy orderly who'd try to grab your cock. Jerking off in the napkins and having fights with them, flung across the ward, the cripples sitting up in bed, silently laughing. Any of these other fucking slobs could have been doing all that. He was a ballplayer. Look at Angus, blind, striking out three out of four. Gibby the bum who couldn't field a popup. And that fake bastard Warren, trying to look good at first, bending into the put-out throw, tense and praying.

Leg would swing. Jerk off in the napkins. Baloney every Sunday night. Soft-boiled eggs like oysters, cold and slimy. The milk was always warm. Leg swinging, he'd balance, applauding, a cigarette easy in his mouth. The fucking jerks!

After a while, he'd hang around Yodel's all he could, arguing sports with Phil, figuring out slugging averages and ERA, handicapping the horses. Nothing at home but always the talk about Special Training. A lotta boys have made a go of it with less to be thankful for than you, Artie. His father would start with that. He was one of the things to be thankful for.

Why not Big Mickey, the fuckin bully?

Little Mickey? So skinny the wind could blow him away.

Fredo the thief?

Donald Duck, the jerk pimply bastard?

Red, who couldn't spell his own name?

Special Training—I saw somethin about it in the *News* last week, Artie. I saw it too, Artie, his mother said. Artie looked out the window at the ailanthus tree in the back yard. His parents sat. SPECIAL TRAINING. It was some magical place that existed between and behind the very letters of the words. You just went downtown somewhere or over to New York and saw somebody about it. The OPA or something. The Home Relief. The OPA had a lot of programs, his father said. All kinds of special programs to help boys. You can't hang around that store all day. I go to school, Artie said, All day. The YMCA, his father said.

At school, Sister Therese Rose told him to pray and to keep himself pure. He did neither. He was a natural. Fuck em all. Fuck God.

FAT PAREZ
Hustle

HE HAD A SLEEPY LOOK, eyes half-closed, mouth loose, like Fink. He would tell them something they didn't know, or didn't really understand, or he would refute something they'd said with information, chapter and verse, out of *Popular Mechanics,* or *Popular Science,* or even *The Reader's Digest.* Very big-time. A smooth scar on his chin, mysterious, a kind of guerdon from some romantic past, his fat ass in corduroy knickers, socks hanging down over Buster Brown bluchers. The others took him as he was and listened or argued. Not as bad as Fink— there was lacking in him that close-held contempt, but essentially they found him insufferable.

He could hit two and a half sewers if he got ahold of the ball, but he fielded badly, too fat. He'd scuttle over and the ball would bounce in front of him and go over his head for extra bases or a home run. So they'd play him at first unless Pep played, who couldn't see well— he'd invariably play first when he played, which wasn't often. Parez made fun of Pep, who always got chosen last, salvaged simply to make the sides even—when he was picked by one of the natural captains before he absolutely had to be, it was worse. Everyone knew it to be a gesture of charity, pity. But he knew he couldn't hit (low liners his speed, with the really bad eye closed he could look down on the ball and scoop it off the ground), and could only take soft, accurate throws to first. Parez would go out in the daisies, louse up his chances, and win the game in the last inning, more often than not, with a blast down the block. The wearying victory of heroes.

Fat banged into a car one day, moving backward to get under a fly that meant the game if it fell fair. His fat ass brushed the car's fender but he was moving too im- placably to stop himself. Unconscious, his head swollen in the back. It was a mild concussion. There was nothing to say to that, a lot of hustle, he'd missed the fly but there it was. Parez lying on the ground, his eyes closed, the teams around him and somebody running to tell his mother. The exact romance of failure. They begrudged him his injury, he used it for months after. In the middle of any maddening sophistry or arrogant reference to a magazine article, there he was for them, cut in air, in the past, right down the street in front of Chicky's house, smashing into that car. The nauseating crack of his head against the car door, his mother screaming and crying, the taxi to the doctor. Hustling, hustling. He shied away from every fly after that, a kind of assumed combat fatigue, resented and respected. One day he said to Pep, I'm tryina *tell* you something, cockeyes! Ac- cepted by everyone, touched by destiny, wounded in ac- tion, above and beyond the call of duty, the mouth opening and snapping shut, cockeyes! the smooth scar on his chin shiny in its mystery.

SENATOR STREET
Colonel Stinky

MOST OF THE ARMY was drafted—shanghaied by the Colonel and one or two trusted lieutenants. If the kids didn't join the army and stay in it after they'd been talked to, Lofter would see to it that the others, completely faithful to him, shunned them. If they didn't, they'd be beaten bare-assed, with a slat from an orange crate.

The swords were of orange-crate slats too, and Lofter, as Colonel, carried a lance made from a red broomstick, red and white ribbons trailing from it, pennons. One said, in blue watercolor, DUTY.

He was older, maybe fifteen, and his troops, twelve strong at one time, were all between nine and twelve. He wore a helmet most of the time, and ran everywhere —cantered, actually, as on a horse. His troops did close-order drill four days a week after school. On the fifth day, they fought, usually on 68th Street.

The Colonel would appear first with a skinny Irish kid, Mikey, his chief lieutenant, both cantering, reconnoitering 68th, checking to see the odds against them. If it looked good, Mikey rode back to Senator, while the Colonel went through some dips and swoops with his lance. Then the army would appear and they'd charge the enemy, flailing with their orange-crate swords, attacking in a column of twos, with five-yard intervals, Stinky at their flanks, exhorting them. For Country, Men! For the Fatherland! For God! The kids attacked would begin by laughing, and then they'd start to kick the hell out of the troops, punching, kneeing, tearing their swords away from them and breaking them across their knees. Once in a while they'd keep a sword as a war prize. They'd try for Stinky's broomstick but he'd be gone after the first assault, leaving his troops on the field for Mikey to take care of and get back around the corner. When he saw them the next day, in the cellar-way HQ, he'd have drawings and maps to show them what they'd done wrong. Sometimes he'd court-martial someone for cowardice. Everyone would punch the convicted soldier on his arms until they were black and blue. Then the Colonel would give a short speech on courage.

He never won a battle, and his troops defected one by one, despite threats and harassments. Mikey started to shoot crap a lot, and Stinky was finally alone. On winter days, after school, he'd stand alone in the lot and go through the Manual of Arms. He'd taken to wearing a swastika on his British helmet, which he'd painted black. Once in a while, some hoods from downtown would chase him home. They thought he was a Jew.

1947

NEW YORK'S FINEST
Cockroach Malone

PATROLMAN THOMAS MALONE, K of C, Emerald Society, Democrat, had been involved in many unorthodox occurrences on his beat.

Sleeping off drunks in broken-into cars.

Disappearing from the streets in times of violence and trouble.

Losing his cap twice, his shield and nightstick once, and his service revolver for three hours. The gun found later under the free-lunch table in Gallagher's.

Uncle Mark a machine ward-boss. Patrolman Malone a more or less average officer, more cocky than most who had to cultivate protection.

Perfect corruption, of the old persuasion, sans St. John's grammar and articulation, desire for betterment, required psychology courses, and Dale Carnegie smiles. Spick, nigger, and dago dear dear words. Also a coward, i.e., he would cover up any action that might invoke the general hostility of his charges. To wit:

A gang of younger boys, loosely grouped together in a social-athletic club, the Senators, had inherited the tradition of the nickel-dime crap game. The Cockroach allowed these games to flourish so long as he got a cut of the money. At times, he would leave his cap, tunic, pistol, and club in Yodel's and play himself, always winning, since the Senators made it a point to bet wrong against him. Of course.

One day, Davy Demonde decided to go, finally, against him and bet with a hot roll that Flynn was on, against Cockroach, who was booking Flynn. Davy gave Cockroach all the odds, but won consistently as Flynn passed again and again. When Cockroach rolled, a few bucks in the hole already, Davy faded him and won when he crapped out. He side-bet him, bet on over and under point with him, beat him at everything. Everybody else laid off, sensing Davy's anger and triumph after all these months.

Malone pulled out of the game after dropping $8.50. He was smiling, grim through his cheap false choppers and blurred alcoholic face, chuckling and calling Davy an assy guinea sonofabitch lucky wop. Ha-ha! All in a spirit of fun. He slapped good ole Davy the wop bastard lucky dago cocksucker greaseball on the back and then went into Yodel's to get into uniform. He walked out, down a few doors and slid into Pat's to make a phone call as an anonymous citizen complaining about a crap game played right on the street—and where were the cops? What the hell did they do all day they can't stop all the gambling and cursing, Jesus Christ!

Outside, he walked to Gallagher's where he found, as he knew he would, Burly, swaying and staggering under his load of Tokay. Whaddayasay, Cockroach, whatsamatta? you look fuckin sober? That's enough shit outa you, Burly, Cockroach said, smiling, I'm makin a pinch on you for drunk an disorderly an insultin an officer in the performance. Cockroach walked to the corner call box, holding his alibi by the elbow.

A couple of minutes later, a squad car pulled up to Yodel's corner, the boys scattered as the bulls charged out, snorting, swinging their nightsticks, scooping up the change on the sidewalk. No bills? No fuckin bills?

1948

EDDY BESHARY
The Box

YOU ARE BOTH MEMBERS of the bovine family, Eddy said. Or perhaps diptera, or lepidoptera. He was standing on one of the paths in Triangle Park, confronting Donato and Azzerini. Donato was laughing, and asked him again, what the fuck you doin with the box, Eddy? For Christ sake, looka the box he got, Tommy. Eddy was holding by the lid a huge cardboard box he had been dragging along the path. Do not trouble yourselves over my eccentricities and my antics as well, Eddy said. My presence in this park is certainly not disturbing you gentlemen? One may, I have long assumed, drag about a cardboard box in broad daylight without incurring the wrath of the authorities, nor the queries of such—*gentlemen* as yourselves. No? You diptera have delayed me.

He's gonna make lists on the box, Donato, Tommy said. And you're gonna be at the bottom, like every year. Most assuredly, Eddy said. Mr. Donato will find himself near the bottom, sharing that place of dubious honor with some choice hooligans from that accursed corner —where, I may say, I no longer hang around. Yeah, where you been, Eddy? Donato said. We miss ya. Don't we miss him, Tommy? We miss ya, Eddy, Tommy said, come back ta the corner, Yodel misses ya, Al Pearson misses ya, everybody misses ya.

Eddy hefted his box and started to walk around them, the box dragging behind him. Ah, Tommy, he said. You had for some time, when you were seriously studying the trombone, found yourself, as you will remember, high up on my annual report to Yodel. But I have heard it rumored that you are now driving a bus, a motorbus, along these corrupt streets. You must, of needs, find yourself close this year to your friend, Mr. Donato, at the bottom of the list, along with some few hooligans as I have mentioned.

What's the matter with drivin a bus? Tommy said, you don't even work at all. Ah, said Eddy, there is no job that will not keep me down at the cellar, the basement, of life. With time to explore my capabilities, I will rise up until one day I will stand on the roof of life, gazing down on you hooligans and wastrels on that corner. I have, you know, known other cities. Paris, Rome, Cairo, women about, beautiful, drinking two glasses of pernod, and perhaps a glass of brandy. But now, I must leave this pleasant conversation with you lepidoptera.

He walked around them and continued on his way,

crossing the street opposite his apartment building and struggling into the lobby, the cardboard box bumping and dragging, as he squeezed it into the door. This guy's a spook, Donato said. *He* don't even know what he's talkin about. Ah, good riddance, Tommy said. Who wants him hangin around the corner playin the banjo on his knuckles? They walked toward the avenue.

1949

THE DOC
The Doctor

THEY CALLED HIM—actually he called himself—the Doc, nobody knew why. He had a beachcomber look, rumpled gabardine suit, tan, brown-and-white scuffed spectators without heels, his shredded imitation Panama. A Hollywood beachcomber doctor, hands shaking from booze, rising to the occasion when a child comes down with beri-beri, and so on. That broken-veined cast of the face and nose.

He drank when and whatever he could, begging, borrowing, wheedling credit. The Doc is a wrong-o, Pepper said, fuck him. He never paid back loans, would stand at the edges of a crap game and bet his dime or quarter on the gunner if he was on a hot roll, then wait until the next hot roll. Then he took to carrying a leather case, a doctor's bag, in fact, and a few weeks later seemed more prosperous. He stood a couple of rounds at the bar, bought Beshary and Al Pearson a few now and again, settled some debts. He got himself a new pair of spectators, stiff cheap leather, and a new hat, a gray felt fedora. The suit stayed the same, but he had it cleaned and pressed. He and Al would discuss the possibilities of atomic power, its use as a fuel for the helicopters that would fly out of the heliport Al would start on the old tennis court next to the lot after he made a killing selling greeting cards.

He had become a fake abortionist, going around with his bag through the Spanish neighborhood downtown, asking around, letting it be known, etc., in pidgin Spanish. He wore a black onyx pinky ring he'd borrowed from Al for these trips. A "professional-looking" ring.

The Doc would take money down on an abortion, rent a cheap hotel room along with the woman to be aborted, and make an appointment to meet her there the next day. He'd give her a couple of aspirins from out of an apothecary bottle dug from his bag, carefully letting the woman see the tools of his trade. The real thing. He'd take whatever she'd give, usually asking fifty dollars— half the total price—but settling sometimes for ten or even five. He had a heart. *Tengo* this *cinco* dollars *porque yo tengo uno grande corazón por* you. *Usted* like *una hermana* to me. *Una hermana.* Then he'd leave, and stay away for a few days, then hit again maybe five blocks away. It was risky, and his story, if he were ever apprehended, was to be that the police had had a secret investigator on him. But nobody ever found him out.

Frank Bull stole his bag one night from the back of the Lion's Den and sold the instruments for fifty dollars. The Doc was in a rage. Fuckin thieves, he said, fuckin sneaky thieves. I got a very good idea who did this and if I ever prove it, he better watch out. He was looking straight at Pete the Sailor, who lifted his leg and farted. Oh Doc, you scarin the shit outa me! Pete said. The Doc turned back to Al and Eddy at the bar. A crude oaf, Eddy said. He never fails to crap out when one has bet with his point: In good faith. *About* the exact meaning of *jeu de mots,* Al said.

BROMO EDDY
The Cab

HE'D HAD a third bromo within the hour and now he was
shaking and blinking furiously. With his hands in his
pockets he could contain the former, but his eyelids
wouldn't keep still and he pulled the vizor of his cap low
so that people wouldn't stare too hard at him. Most who
didn't know him stared anyway, and many passengers
had nervously cut their rides in his cab short of their
destinations after looking a few minutes in the rear-
view mirror at Eddy's eyes, closed, it seemed, more
often than not.

He started down 69th again to circle the block once
more. Maybe Mario took the cab, or Pete the Sailor, as
a joke. He'd left the keys in when he went into the Royal
for coffee, and now the damn cab was gone. But it would
show up, sure show up. Nobody would take a cab! Really
take a cab, like *steal* it. What could anybody do with a
cab, beat up, the transmission shot, grinding gears. A
cab.

Now it was two o'clock and Eddy sat at the bar in
Gallagher's having a Fleischmann's and ginger. He'd
given up on the cab and total despair was settling on
him. Keys in the ignition, the doors unlocked, the company's cab—gone. He had a record, the bulls would be
around right away, questions, looking for an angle. Well,
Eddy, that your name, Eddy? do you know anybody who
might wanna *borrow* a cab for sumpn? A little outing?
A joyride? It would start. Oh, your record, yeah. Car

theft, first offense. Oh, car theft, hah? You were a kid then, right? Just foolin around. Joyridin.

But he'd call the company first, tell them, get that in anyway, nice and straight, and then let the bulls come in on it. Fuck the Cockroach, that drunk Irish bastard would love to give him a hard time on his own, first, nice and easy, rub it in. Ya blink so fuckin much anyway, Eddy, ya can't see what's happenin anyway. Maybe you were lookin right at the cab an didn't see it float away? Maybe it *floated* away?

At three thirty, he still hadn't called and Pepper came in the bar. Hey Eddy B! I'll buy ya drink, he said. I got my disability today—you look kinda fucked up. What's up? He told Pepper and they drank. At four, Pete the Sailor came in. Eddy kid, ya cab's a fuckin wreck. Konik smashed it up against a lamppost on 8oth Street, he musta been drunk—Jesus Christ, Eddy, why you let Konik take ya cab? He ain't got *no* kinda license at all. Eddy was looking at Pete, cold and numb. Konik? In my cab? You betcher ass it's your cab, the cops're lookin for ya, ya better call em. Didja know the short was gone? I knew, Eddy said. He drank his shot and then sipped at the ginger. Too late now, fool around, and around, and now too late. Don't call us, he said, we'll call you. Who? Pete said. What the hell was Konik doin on 8oth Street? Eddy said. Didn't he useta live up that way when he was a kid? Pepper said. Christ knows, Eddy said. He took a dime off the bar. I'm gonna report the cab missin to the compny. What a laugh that'll be. He looked as if he had bitten into a lemon.

1946

THE POOLROOM

BIG AL and Coney Island Mike were playing a game of straight pool, 150 points, for a straight 250 dollars. No dime a ball or anything like that, just the flat sum of money, no spot, since they were both very good shots, certainly the best in Sal's. Al was a baker and used to play pool all the time he wasn't in the bakery, and nobody knew what Coney Island Mike did. He was a small man, gray and wizened, and he always wore a dark-gray hat and smoked a cigar. He shot pool in a vest and he kept his hat on. Al was a big Pole and would shoot in his undershirt, with a special stick that Sal kept locked up in a small cabinet. Mike always carried his stick with him, in two pieces, in a little chipped and scarred leather case.

They shot very differently. Al took wild chances to break the rack, then he could run out fifty or sixty balls at a time with ease; he almost always missed the same kind of shot that he had made to initiate his run: it wasn't overconfidence or carelessness, he just took each shot a little faster than the one before, until finally he stepped on his own rhythm and got off his stroke, then missed. Mike was a snooker player, waited a half hour for the right shot, if he didn't have it he'd safe, safe, so that he'd force Al into taking that one wild shot—Mike would gamble that Al would miss and break the rack for him: if he didn't miss, then Mike knew he'd be down those fifty or so points. When Mike broke the rack for himself, he'd take each shot methodically, judging it, setting up his position exactly, so that he'd have as little trouble as possible with his next ball. He would miss after a run of about the same amount as Al's, and most of the time because of bad position—he'd be pressured into making a grandstand shot that he had never planned on having to make.

This night, Al was shooting and in the middle of a run; he'd just sunk his rack and the last ball was poised perfectly at the edge of the truncated triangle of new balls as Sal racked them on the table. Mike was ahead, 110 to 95, but Al was shooting beautifully now, and it looked as if Mike would lose for certain. The balls racked, Al shot, sinking the loose ball in the corner pocket, smashing the rack, the cue ball skidding with its strong english through the slowly spreading balls, battering them apart, caroming off the rails, and finally coming to rest in the center of the table, the rack spread open, the balls distinct, with plenty of air between them.

He'd put away about half the rack when he took a ridiculous chance and tried a side pocket shot that was a sure scratch unless the cue ball had enough english on it to pull it away from the corner pocket; it was an unnecessary shot, because Al really had plums all over the table, but nobody was surprised when he took it, and nobody was surprised when he scratched. He'd put the english on the cue all right, but there was a ball at the lip of the corner pocket which acted as a deflector for the cue ball, and it went in for his scratch.

Mike had the game made now. Only 40 points to make, and the table open before him, something that you simply could not do with a position player like Mike. He sank the rank, broke the next one with his opening shot, and Al sat down, shaking his head. He always shook his head when he left the table open after a missed, unnecessary shot. Everybody felt bad for Al, not only because he was the neighborhood ace, but because he played with a kind of bravura, a romanticism that all the young pool players admired. They were a little put off, a little frightened by Mike, whose precision, just because it was so conscious and premeditated, seemed to them unfair.

Mike had about six balls to go for game and was moving implacably through the last rack of balls. Somebody down in the corner was arguing with Fat George about keeping two feet on the floor, and his voice was getting louder and louder. It was, as everybody immediately knew, Dick Tracy, a would-be hustler, who always wore a wide-brimmed pearl gray hat down over one eye, and shot pool with a cigarette dangling out of his mouth, the smoke curling into his eyes, billowing under the brim of his hat. He was a big Chicago and Acey-Five player with the younger boys in the poolroom, knowing just enough about the game to beat them out of their nickels and dimes. He would never play with the good shots, and if by some chance he was pushed into a money-ball game with them, he'd sweat and weep about how he'd lost his stroke, how he didn't have his good stick.

His voice got louder and louder as Mike concentrated on the last ball for score. He was almost shrieking at George then, as Mike took his last shot, a bridge shot, and as Mike shot, Dick Tracy banged his cue on the floor with a heavy thump. Mike's stick glanced off the cue ball and it skittered away, harmlessly, on the felt. Mike looked at it, then bent down, put the bridge under the table, and started to screw his cue stick apart. Al sat and looked at him as Sal racked up his points—148—then Mike walked over to Al and handed him a roll of bills. Here, Al, he said. No sense in tiring yourself. I blew it. Al took the money, but wouldn't look at Mike. Mike put his stick into the leather case, took care of the time with Sal, and walked out. Dick Tracy had apparently won his argument with Fat George, and was now bent over the table, stroking—the smoke from his cigarette moving in eddies under his hat brim—for the ten-cent five ball. Sal sent one of the kids down to the Royal for a container of soup.

DICK TRACY
The Exposé

THE GLORIOUS NIGHT that Fat George revealed the man! Whatever his name was, Nick or Jimmy, some bread-truck driver with flat feet or some other million-dollar deferment. Asthma. Everyone knew him as Dick Tracy, his wide-brimmed slouch hat, over his right eye, pulled so low that half his face was masked. The omnipresent cigarette. He growled, he cursed, he looked over the balls on the table, muttering english secrets to himself, bank angles, combinations. The young players stood in awe of him.

The feeling was clear in the poolroom that, despite this brilliant display of presence by Dick Tracy, almost anybody could beat him. But nobody beat him. The whole of him was too much to combat. He was out of a movie, he was what all the boys expected to find in the poolroom. So he won. When some kid dropped in a beautiful shot, Dick Tracy would scowl and grimace. Sometimes he'd grin and slowly shake his head, grinding his butt out on the floor, softly tapping the end of his cue stick, looking up to heaven. Ah, it was against all the laws of God to beat this man.

One night Fat George, swinging and swaying his hips to help a money ball into the corner pocket, turned so that the tip of his cue caught under Dick Tracy's hat brim and swept his hat off. The boys looked, all games stopped. Dick Tracy was bald. He was an old man, bald, helpless-looking and ludicrous, with his cigarette ridiculous in that defenseless face. He groped on the floor for his hat, grumbling and swearing at George, then sensed the stillness: everyone looking. Then the laughter. He put his hat on. Well, well, Dick Tracy, Dickie Tracy, George said. I'm fucked! Dick *Tracy!* He had his hat on again in an instant, scowling, scowling. The whole poolroom loud with laughter. Sad and just.

1950

KONIK
Doing It In

HE HAD FORGOTTEN his name and his hands were numb at the fingertips. They tingled with pins and needles as if he had awakened from a sleep in which his arm had been trapped beneath his body. That too seemed numb and heavy and he simply allowed it to carry him forward—it knew what was happening and what to do. To his eye, everything was startlingly familiar, he swore that he still lived in this building with them, their follies and strait, boring cruelties.

Eddy's cab was parked carefully at the curb. He wore his cap over one eye, as Eddy did. He reached down and lifted the hall rug up, then peeled it back from the gray felt mat beneath and there was the key. His hand put it toward the keyhole, and in it, and the door opened.

He walked in and to the front window to look out at the cab. It seemed very clear there in the sunlight. Very permanent. Then he walked back to the door and closed it, and sat down on a straight chair in the living room. He was sweating and vaguely nauseous and could smell spareribs and cabbage cooking, the smell stronger from the kitchen as he approached it. There was nothing cooking in the kitchen, but that familiar Monday night smell, which he loathed, was intense. In his eye: navy beans with cider vinegar: Jell-O, a cracked brown bowl half-full, the rubbery surface, skinlike: weak tea: Woolworth cookies, rectangular, speckled with granulated sugar, a clear "W" in a diamond in the center. He smelled greasy filet of sole.

He got up from the kitchen chair and walked back to the living room—in *that* corner of what had been called then the "front room" he had slept on a lumpy three-cushioned couch. There was a sofa-bed there. He looked at his hand and at the chef's knife it held loosely. Then he carefully began to cut the sofa-bed to pieces. Then the easy chairs. The straight chairs he gutted, then with the back of the knife blade pried the ornamental upholsterer's tacks out and piled them on the coffee table. He took the pictures down and placed them on the floor, then smashed the glass in them with his heel. In the kitchen he emptied all the cupboards and cabinets and the refrigerator of their food, then dumped it all in the middle of the floor, meticulously emptying each box. He opened each can and when necessary scooped out the contents with a spoon. The spoon he wiped on the crisp kitchen curtains.

In the bedroom his body lost control for a second and he put his foot through a window, but broke only one pane, cleanly. The glass tinkled slightly, a few shards falling to the alley bordering the side of the house. He went into the bathroom and shit in the sink then picked up the ordure with wads of toilet paper and, starting at the front door, smeared it all over the walls. In the bedroom he wrote with the clotted and filthy toilet paper, scrubbing the words onto the white wall: UNCLE JIM AUNT EDITH DEAD BASTARDS. He washed his hands and face and left, locking the door and placing the key in its hiding place, then walked to Eddy's cab. He let his body drive the cab away, a smile floating across his face, from eyes to mouth, then passing off, in wave after wave, dreamily.

1941

MOVIE HOUSES

THEY WENT to the Alpine because it was there. Built as a "palace," but without a balcony, to discourage fornication and prevent smoking. The children's section was a zoo, manic and insanely loud. Red's girl was straddling him in the Bay Ridge balcony, her dress up around her waist when they put the lights on to collect for the Defense Effort. You got flea and louse bites in the Stanley: that was the Itch.

The Stanley was for Sunday. Gibby was there with his mother when Pearl Harbor was attacked. They *stopped* the picture so the manager could tell the audience. The last row of seats in the Electra's balcony had the armrests ripped out by lovers. One long couch. They gave dishes away there on Wednesday nights. The Sunset was a bucket of blood, filled with junior members of downtown gangs. They threw bottles at scenes they didn't like. The matrons quit every Saturday. Your mother took you to the Fortway to see Clark Gable and Bette Davis, fuck them.

The Stanley had wooden seats that creaked and the picture flickered and ran off the reel every show. They had a candy machine in there. The Alpine had a counter and a men's room with a lounge where the kids stood and smoked Wings and Twenty Grands. The Dyker was for Friday night, all boys save only the bravest of girls. It was loud and obscene. Many boys got drunk for the first time in that famous balcony: on muscatel and sherry. On Friday nights you could hear the bottles clanking down the steps.

The Electra showed pictures nobody ever heard of: *The White Gorilla*. People like Bruce Cabot and Tim Holt were in their hapless footage, strung together with old travelogues, the audience yelled and screamed for their money back, but they didn't want their money back. It was the style of going to the Electra. Sunday afternoons in the Alpine were respectable with families and kids drooling over their Charms.

The Fortway was somewhere to hell and gone, nobody ever remembered its decor. The Dyker was a trip on the trolley or a long walk. A really different neighborhood, people had money there. They got the "new" pictures. Right from New York. The Stanley showed endless coming attractions. Mon-Tues. Wed-Thurs. Fri-Sat-Sun. The whole neighborhood saw George Raft flip his coin into death there.

The Bay Ridge was so dark you really could get laid there. It was huge and full of corridors and stairways, gold leaf and velvet chairs, long fake Persian runners. The dark corners were alive with passion. The boys raged and roared at some chooch named Victor Mature. What a *fuckin* name! Victor Ma-CHOOR! The lovers oblivious in the dark, sighs, release, ah God, so sweet, safe from the cold streets.

You got colds, rheumatism, arthritis, bronchitis, pneumonia, from the air-conditioning in the Alpine—the pioneers. It was absolutely frigid, great blasts of icy air swept over the audience from June to September, it was delicious. In July, kids stood outside the doors to get the whiffs of chilled air as patrons went in and out. It was the only place you could successfully sneak into.

In the Bay Ridge everybody followed the bouncing ball. In the Electra. The flag waved. The *March of Time* showed everybody what a prick Hitler was. Mussolini was not too much of a prick. The Finns beat the shit out of the Russians. God won in Spain over those Red bastards who fucked nuns and pissed on the crucifix.

1950

THE LIST

AN ANNUAL LISTING, by Eddy Beshary, according to excellence, of all those who gathered in Yodel's store. Hugely and painstakingly lettered in pen, pencil, and red crayon on 8½ x 11 blank white sheets Scotch-taped together to form a scroll and illuminated throughout by drawings, newspaper clippings, photographs, and Arabic scrawls, it was a numbered roll of names, each followed by a comment, which to Eddy served as explanation and reason for the place of rank. The list was read aloud to Yodel by Eddy in the store, and then presented to him as a gift.

1. *Al Pearson*—A man of great genius little understood by the rabble. He has scored more bon mots than any living Frenchman. Dr. Pearson is his nom dee plume.
2. *Philip Yodel*—Since Philip is my patron and protector I must say that he is a scholarly gentleman of high repute. However he reads too, much, about the Earthworm sports of this Country of bovines.
   (Drawing of newspaper with headlines reading: DUKE SNIDER DEAD. COWS WEEP.)
3. *Gibby*—A young man of great promise who reads

many books. He engages Dr. Pearson in multifarius level conversation also he knows how to spell Parchesi four different ways all, of which are, Correct!!!!

4. *Kenny*—A vision of sortarial splendor, plus intelligence. He instantly knew the difference between a coaster and a caster when questioned.

5. *Whitey the Greek*—A reserved and dignified young man who dresses neatly and with taste. One pictures him speaking with beautiful woman in the cafés of Istanbul and Teheran.

6. *Jake Collom*—A young man with strong social views. A chemist who uses algebra and arithmetics with impunity, and x's and y's. An attendant of college. He makes fun of Dr. Pearson however but this lack of respect can be attributed to his youth.
(Clipping of baby wearing a top hat and a sash with 1950 lettered on it. Balloon drawn by Eddy from baby's mouth has a line in Arabic over a line of x's and y's.)

7. *Donnie G.*—I have noticed him with tomes. But his nauseating name G keeps him from higher ranking. (Cutout of girl in bikini in cheesecake pose. Her balloon says, "Gee!")

8. *Artie Salvo*—Due to his unfortunate physical liability he makes it a practice to congregate with the various specys of diptera and ephemeroptera who frequent the Billiard academy. His accounting studies give him some sanguinaries.

9. *Carmine*—A man who plays regularly on a tenor saxophone. He has a lovely young ladyfriend and I understand that he attends the college at night. He spends too much time with such pocket billiard devotes as Fat George the Armenian equine.

10. *Black Mac*—I do not know this Irish gentleman although I understand him to associate at times with Gibby and Kenny. He appears like a roughly polish diptera.

11. *George Berl*—I do not know this gentleman either but he has a large ass.
12. *Pepper*—A man who eats all the free lunch in the saloon while quaffing perhaps two glasses of beer. A rapacious canine who after, drinks himself into a stupor at home. Also his front teeth are missing so that he is want to spit all over your newly cleaned suit as he engages you in conversation. A Boston bulldog.
13. *Pete the Sailor*—All sailors should be exiled to Albania. Mr. Peter Sailor should be sent to the coal mines there. A gentleman who cannot shoot craps. Even his stattus is thirteen.
    (Drawing of dice with two spots up. Next to it the words, "crapped out.")
14. *Paul Camden*—A still barrel sounds hollow.
15. *Fat George*—A fat Armenian lad who lets his father's Greek olives shrivel up in the Billiard academy as he loses his money playing very very bad games of Acey-Five.
16. *Red Mulvaney*—Eamon de Valera needs this type to bury Ireland forever and make Man-kind happy. A man of little musical knowledge. An excellent chance to grow into an officer of the law or another type of petty criminal.
17. *Red——?*—A tall scandinavian or celtic. Undistinguished.
18. *Leo Fink*—I do not know this gentleman too well but he talks like a man with a paper asshole. Is he some kind of soldier? If so, he must be put at the bottom of the list below even the orangootang Donato.
19. *Donald Duck*—A mechanic of such ilk as Fords and Chevrolettes. I feel a malaize to look at his greasy trousers.
20. *Eddy Bromo*—A man with the IQ of a cabdriver. He is a cabdriver. He thinks that Fords and Chevrolettes are automobiles like greasy Duckie. Also he blinks his

eyes too much while he clutters Yodel's fountain with his discarded and useless bromo seltzer glasses. He is a dope addict to this ameba's beverage.

(Drawing of a counter cluttered with Bromo-Seltzer glasses, all of which bear a skull and crossbones and the words BROMO SELTZER.)

21. *Gus Makaros*—A Greek who smokes cheap cigars and gives honest gentlemen like myself a headache with his hyena laugh. I understand that his presence in the armed forces was the cause of the battle of the Bulge.

22. *Joe Kane*—A Don Juan whose greatest conquest is his own wee-wee. He associates with the Greek, Makaros. He smokes cigars and laughs like a hyena but also has a fat ass.

23. *Burly*—An alcoholic disaster area, an atomic bomb fell on him at his birth. This is a type of man who lives in the coalbin and eats vanella Mello-Rolls.

24. *The Doc*—A faker and a phony. He owes me personally for three glasses of whiskey and four glasses of beer.

(Drawing of dollar bill with wings.)

25. *Fat Phil*—A Greek who might someday if he is lucky learn to repair Fords and Chevrolettes.

26. *Frank Bull*—A credit to his race.

(Drawing of a gorilla holding a flag which says: DON'T STEP ON ME.)

27. *Pat Glade*—A drunkard who watches the foolishness of baseball and feetball on Television. Also works for Civil Service which ranks him as an automatic bovine. He will always remain in the bomb shelter of the house of Success.

28. *Artie Shaerbach*—A mistake of Momma Nature. A Hooligan.

29. *Doc*—I do not know this ephemeroptera who jumps out of airaplanes. A canine member.

(Clipping of a dog smoking a cigar.)

30. *Jimmy Lately*—A garbage man if he studies at night.
(Clipping of Mayor O'Dwyer smiling as he awards a scroll for meritorious service to an Eagle Scout. On the scroll Eddie has written: EXCELLENT GARBAGE.)

31. *Roy Dobbs*—He will also make an excellent garbage man when he grows up at seventy.

32. *Johnny Dobbs*—He speaks with the voice of an angel.
(Drawing of angel with balloon saying F——YOU!)

33. *Sprenger*—This is an insane diptera. A hallucinationary coleoptera.

34. *Thom. Azzerini*—This pitiful crustacean is a bus driver. One would like to place him at the bottom of the list except that honor goes to his deaf and dumb lobster friend Donato.

35. *Donato*—Last heard from throwing around giant fardels of coffee for Maxwell house. He resides alone at the bottom of the list and below the Bomb shelter. A crawfish on Holidays.

1944

BESHARYISM
First Exposition: To a Bartender

IN ANY LIFE, dozens of mishaps will occur. Man is thrust under by waves of misfortune, drowned and filled with poisoned gallons of water, little fish and varied crustaceans inhabit his body and eat him all up. This cannot be helped. But some mishaps occur because man refuses to raise himself above the level of the common housefly, Musca domestic. A lowly diptera. He grovels in the pit, chasing wealth, refusing to glance to right or left in his running around like a crazy sheep. Higher wisdom and joy is unknown to him, while he runs after the greenbacks. When he has his hands filled with them, he runs after more, and even more, until he goes crazy from greed. And where is he anyway?—down in the basement, down in the cellar! Devoided of culture and spiritual harmony. This is true. He may think he is happy, the lout arachnida, chasing after women, fucking them! But as he grows older he realizes that the true meanings of life have passed him by and that he is, after all, just a fucking jester, a Pagliacci. Oh, how bitter he laughs then, how he calls on Jesus and whoever else, his old gray-haired mama, his slavey wife, and his juvenile delinquent hooligan children to take pity on him. But they are all down in the basement with him, chasing the greenbacks too. So menkind must get out of that basement to be happy, get away from these menial tasks he thinks are okay. Because they are *not* okay! The improvement of the mind, the richness of reading the dictionary to express yourself, books on how to identify floras and faunas—all these things are okay! All these things are the key to get you out of the basement and up to the higher floors—to the roof, the penthouse! Money is nothing without culture and learning, who cares about a new suit on a stupid back? But old raggedy clothes from the Salvation Army on a smart back, on the back of the man on the roof!—they are like gold cloth and jewels! How many floors there are, even I can't guess, but it's high, the building is high, and not many of the crawly cockaroaches can make it up even the first flight, running after dollars and their simple thrills of whiskey and beer and gin and women who laugh at them with those white teeth that they have—and big breasts thrusted out at them. How can a man study and learn? The cockaroaches laugh and hang on the corner like loathsome beetles, or crickets, unliterate son of a

bitches! On the first floor are undubitably, are the cockaroaches and crickets, along with bovine creatures and
jellyfishes. Great winds blow the greenbacks around!
They scottle after them. They fight with tooth and by
nails and pincers and horns for these bucks, and stay on
the floor. The next few floors are filled and repleted with
diptera and coleoptera and felines, big canines and lob-
sters. Some of these people can spell a little. These animals and strange crustaceans. They know the
difference between a coaster and a caster, many have
gone to school which they have wasted feeling girls'
chests and buttocks and spending their money on rubbers and dirty books of ladies in their underwear.
Wasted their youth. They remember a few little things
which get them menial jobs in large companies and
they drink their cocktails. Love of beautiful, cultured
women is unknown to them, they are content with some
neighborhood slattern who will cook them their ham
and eggs and stews and some canned butter beans for
Sunday. They clank around in bedroom slippers on these
floors and they feel superior to the cockaraoches underneath them, for they have conquered a few pennies.
Higher up, now we can see some sunshine coming
through the windows, forcing through the grimy . . . shit,
on their windows. Up here are varied species of equines
and God knows what glowworms and ephemeroptera
and water spiders, with good clothes and magazine sub-
scriptions. They brush their teeth every morning so
their wives will love them. They are dopey. They don't
know that just a few more flights and they'll be on the
roof with the human men, strong men, with clear eyes
who have said the shit with the greenbacks and tooth-
paste and all that other effluvia. What do they do, reading their magazines? They see clothes to buy. Like a
bunch of formicas, they follow each other to the cloth-
ing store, and buy their GGG and Hickey-Freeman and

Crawford suits, and slacks, and sport shirts and Adam hats. They are full of pride and shit. On the weekend they copulate their wives a couple of times, and read the *News.* And above them, their eyes in the stars, are the men of the world, strolling about, looking down at the hot, dirty city, beautiful, cultured women hanging from their arms, whispering philosophy to them, hugging them once in a while in light moments. Once in a while some pesky fuck diptera or a cockaroach happens to come by by accident and they just flit them, squirt-squirt and go on with their discussion. Down on the corner the animal families talk with the other animals and flying creatures about baseball or playing pinochle. You can look down and see them in the grime and garbage from the roof. It is all blue and bright up there and you kiss your cultured paramour underneath the moon.

1947

BURLEYCUE
Phil

THAT HE KNEW the size of every stripper's breasts in Union City did not prevent him from weeping in the night, greasy-sweated in his bed: that he knew all the jokes of all the comics (which he enjoyed but went to pant at the strippers and jerk off with his hand in his pocket surrounded by other men, delirious in their lust).

A connoisseur of the art who went every Friday night, the long trip to catch an old favorite. Lily St. Cyr or Tempest Fury. Once she looked right at him and put out her tongue, moved it in a slow circle around her lips. Looking at him! His scalp got hot and prickled and he knew she saw him rubbing himself under his overcoat and hat.

Some had bells and tassels. Some had net stockings and jeweled garters. Some fucked the curtains, some an imaginary man on top of a little cocktail table, drunk on martinis. That was some kind of fancy drink you drank when you were rich. He would stare at his stiff cock, the skinny white legs tense on his sheets. It would be somebody else's hand. Would no one care for him? His *brother* got married!

They moved to "Temptation," "A Pretty Girl," "Alice Blue Gown," "I'm a Big Girl Now," "A Good Man is Hard to Find." They bumped, they ground, they did splits. The men trembled and laughed, tight, at the rusty comic routines they knew by heart, while they ogled the nurse, the receptionist, the prisoner, the maid, the rich matron, the lady canvasser. Phil thought of these skits more than anything else, for they wore no costumes, but clothes. Clothes! Underneath them they had on underwear! Real girls' underwear. They were real! It was unbearable.

If you could get a real woman to do a strip! A woman in the street, any woman! He groaned in his bed and looked at the sports pages. He couldn't do it again, it was four o'clock in the morning, he had to get up at six. But what would he do?

He joked about it with clenched teeth. He went alone, always. He went straight home and sat down in his easy chair, trembling. Once he began to weep in the Hudson Tubes. He could feel the soft flesh of thighs under his hands and sat on them, grinding the palms into the varnished straw of the seat, his head bent, the tears dropping off his chin and jaws into the grime and dust of the floor. Then his hands went to sleep.

THE LOT

IT WAS BITTER COLD, the light was dying fast over the bay to the boy's left, and he hunched closer to the fire, stirring and poking at the mickeys black and charred in the center of the roaring embers. The lot was empty, all the other kids gone home long ago—his mother would kill him when he got in, but he had to eat these mickeys, even if he had to eat them alone. Across the street, the entrance to the park was choked with bulldozers, cranes, heaps of rock and brick and soil, where they were tearing out a gigantic strip of grass and trees to make a highway to connect with the new parkway going through along the bay, and then out the length of Long Island. It was sad to see the park going like that, the tunnels would soon have highway streaking under them, instead of the old, cobbled walks he knew. One crane stood harsh silhouetted against the sky, and he stretched his hands out toward the fire. It was almost completely dark now, and he looked behind him, across the lot, to see if anyway someone was there. But there was nobody. The wind blew the dust up in swirls and then straight across the lot at him. He turned his back to it and listened to the fire scream and sing as the blast hit it, the mickeys split in two now, snow-white meat bursting out from the thick char of skin. He pushed his stick into them, one after the other, and lifted them from the fire, smoking. It began to snow.

"They are all gone into the world of light"

SELECTED DALKEY ARCHIVE TITLES

PETROS ABATZOGLOU, *What Does Mrs. Freeman Want?*
MICHAL AJVAZ, *The Golden Age.*
The Other City.
PIERRE ALBERT-BIROT, *Grabinoulor.*
YUZ ALESHKOVSKY, *Kangaroo.*
FELIPE ALFAU, *Chromos.*
Locos.
JOÃO ALMINO, *The Book of Emotions.*
IVAN ÂNGELO, *The Celebration.*
The Tower of Glass.
DAVID ANTIN, *Talking.*
ANTÓNIO LOBO ANTUNES, *Knowledge of Hell.*
The Splendor of Portugal.
ALAIN ARIAS-MISSON, *Theatre of Incest.*
IFTIKHAR ARIF AND WAQAS KHWAJA, EDS., *Modern Poetry of Pakistan.*
JOHN ASHBERY AND JAMES SCHUYLER, *A Nest of Ninnies.*
ROBERT ASHLEY, *Perfect Lives.*
GABRIELA AVIGUR-ROTEM, *Heatwave and Crazy Birds.*
HEIMRAD BÄCKER, *transcript.*
DJUNA BARNES, *Ladies Almanack.*
Ryder.
JOHN BARTH, *LETTERS.*
Sabbatical.
DONALD BARTHELME, *The King.*
Paradise.
SVETISLAV BASARA, *Chinese Letter.*
MIQUEL BAUÇÀ, *The Siege in the Room.*
RENÉ BELLETTO, *Dying.*
MAREK BIEŃCZYK, *Transparency.*
MARK BINELLI, *Sacco and Vanzetti Must Die!*
ANDREI BITOV, *Pushkin House.*
ANDREJ BLATNIK, *You Do Understand.*
LOUIS PAUL BOON, *Chapel Road.*
My Little War.
Summer in Termuren.
ROGER BOYLAN, *Killoyle.*
IGNÁCIO DE LOYOLA BRANDÃO, *Anonymous Celebrity.*
The Good-Bye Angel.
Teeth under the Sun.
Zero.
BONNIE BREMSER, *Troia: Mexican Memoirs.*
CHRISTINE BROOKE-ROSE, *Amalgamemnon.*
BRIGID BROPHY, *In Transit.*
MEREDITH BROSNAN, *Mr. Dynamite.*
GERALD L. BRUNS, *Modern Poetry and the Idea of Language.*
EVGENY BUNIMOVICH AND J. KATES, EDS., *Contemporary Russian Poetry: An Anthology.*
GABRIELLE BURTON, *Heartbreak Hotel.*
MICHEL BUTOR, *Degrees.*
Mobile.
Portrait of the Artist as a Young Ape.
G. CABRERA INFANTE, *Infante's Inferno.*
Three Trapped Tigers.
JULIETA CAMPOS, *The Fear of Losing Eurydice.*
ANNE CARSON, *Eros the Bittersweet.*
ORLY CASTEL-BLOOM, *Dolly City.*
CAMILO JOSÉ CELA, *Christ versus Arizona.*
The Family of Pascual Duarte.
The Hive.
LOUIS-FERDINAND CÉLINE, *Castle to Castle.*
Conversations with Professor Y.
London Bridge.

Normance.
North.
Rigadoon.
MARIE CHAIX, *The Laurels of Lake Constance.*
HUGO CHARTERIS, *The Tide Is Right.*
JEROME CHARYN, *The Tar Baby.*
ERIC CHEVILLARD, *Demolishing Nisard.*
LUIS CHITARRONI, *The No Variations.*
MARC CHOLODENKO, *Mordechai Schamz.*
JOSHUA COHEN, *Witz.*
EMILY HOLMES COLEMAN, *The Shutter of Snow.*
ROBERT COOVER, *A Night at the Movies.*
STANLEY CRAWFORD, *Log of the S.S. The Mrs Unguentine.*
Some Instructions to My Wife.
ROBERT CREELEY, *Collected Prose.*
RENÉ CREVEL, *Putting My Foot in It.*
RALPH CUSACK, *Cadenza.*
SUSAN DAITCH, *L.C.*
Storytown.
NICHOLAS DELBANCO, *The Count of Concord.*
Sherbrookes.
NIGEL DENNIS, *Cards of Identity.*
PETER DIMOCK, *A Short Rhetoric for Leaving the Family.*
ARIEL DORFMAN, *Konfidenz.*
COLEMAN DOWELL, *The Houses of Children.*
Island People.
Too Much Flesh and Jabez.
ARKADII DRAGOMOSHCHENKO, *Dust.*
RIKKI DUCORNET, *The Complete Butcher's Tales.*
The Fountains of Neptune.
The Jade Cabinet.
The One Marvelous Thing.
Phosphor in Dreamland.
The Stain.
The Word "Desire."
WILLIAM EASTLAKE, *The Bamboo Bed.*
Castle Keep.
Lyric of the Circle Heart.
JEAN ECHENOZ, *Chopin's Move.*
STANLEY ELKIN, *A Bad Man.*
Boswell: A Modern Comedy.
Criers and Kibitzers, Kibitzers and Criers.
The Dick Gibson Show.
The Franchiser.
George Mills.
The Living End.
The MacGuffin.
The Magic Kingdom.
Mrs. Ted Bliss.
The Rabbi of Lud.
Van Gogh's Room at Arles.
FRANÇOIS EMMANUEL, *Invitation to a Voyage.*
ANNIE ERNAUX, *Cleaned Out.*
SALVADOR ESPRIU, *Ariadne in the Grotesque Labyrinth.*
LAUREN FAIRBANKS, *Muzzle Thyself.*
Sister Carrie.
LESLIE A. FIEDLER, *Love and Death in the American Novel.*
JUAN FILLOY, *Faction.*
Op Oloop.
ANDY FITCH, *Pop Poetics.*
GUSTAVE FLAUBERT, *Bouvard and Pécuchet.*
KASS FLEISHER, *Talking out of School.*

FORD MADOX FORD,
  The March of Literature.
JON FOSSE, *Aliss at the Fire.*
  Melancholy.
MAX FRISCH, *I'm Not Stiller.*
  Man in the Holocene.
CARLOS FUENTES, *Christopher Unborn.*
  Distant Relations.
  Terra Nostra.
  Vlad.
  Where the Air Is Clear.
TAKEHIKO FUKUNAGA, *Flowers of Grass.*
WILLIAM GADDIS, *J R.*
  The Recognitions.
JANICE GALLOWAY, *Foreign Parts.*
  The Trick Is to Keep Breathing.
WILLIAM H. GASS, *Cartesian Sonata
    and Other Novellas.*
  Finding a Form.
  A Temple of Texts.
  The Tunnel.
  Willie Masters' Lonesome Wife.
GÉRARD GAVARRY, *Hoppla! 1 2 3.*
  Making a Novel.
ETIENNE GILSON,
  The Arts of the Beautiful.
  Forms and Substances in the Arts.
C. S. GISCOMBE, *Giscome Road.*
  Here.
  Prairie Style.
DOUGLAS GLOVER, *Bad News of the Heart.*
  The Enamoured Knight.
WITOLD GOMBROWICZ,
  A Kind of Testament.
PAULO EMÍLIO SALES GOMES, *P's Three
    Women.*
KAREN ELIZABETH GORDON, *The Red Shoes.*
GEORGI GOSPODINOV, *Natural Novel.*
JUAN GOYTISOLO, *Count Julian.*
  Exiled from Almost Everywhere.
  Juan the Landless.
  Makbara.
  Marks of Identity.
PATRICK GRAINVILLE, *The Cave of Heaven.*
HENRY GREEN, *Back.*
  Blindness.
  Concluding.
  Doting.
  Nothing.
JACK GREEN, *Fire the Bastards!*
JIŘÍ GRUŠA, *The Questionnaire.*
GABRIEL GUDDING,
  Rhode Island Notebook.
MELA HARTWIG, *Am I a Redundant
    Human Being?*
JOHN HAWKES, *The Passion Artist.*
  Whistlejacket.
ELIZABETH HEIGHWAY, ED., *Contemporary
    Georgian Fiction.*
ALEKSANDAR HEMON, ED.,
  Best European Fiction.
AIDAN HIGGINS, *Balcony of Europe.*
  A Bestiary.
  Blind Man's Bluff
  Bornholm Night-Ferry.
  Darkling Plain: Texts for the Air.
  Flotsam and Jetsam.
  Langrishe, Go Down.
  Scenes from a Receding Past.
  Windy Arbours.
KEIZO HINO, *Isle of Dreams.*
KAZUSHI HOSAKA, *Plainsong.*

ALDOUS HUXLEY, *Antic Hay.*
  Crome Yellow.
  Point Counter Point.
  Those Barren Leaves.
  Time Must Have a Stop.
NAOYUKI II, *The Shadow of a Blue Cat.*
MIKHAIL IOSSEL AND JEFF PARKER, EDS.,
  *Amerika: Russian Writers View the
    United States.*
DRAGO JANČAR, *The Galley Slave.*
GERT JONKE, *The Distant Sound.*
  Geometric Regional Novel.
  Homage to Czerny.
  The System of Vienna.
JACQUES JOUET, *Mountain R.*
  Savage.
  Upstaged.
CHARLES JULIET, *Conversations with
    Samuel Beckett and Bram van
    Velde.*
MIEKO KANAI, *The Word Book.*
YORAM KANIUK, *Life on Sandpaper.*
HUGH KENNER, *The Counterfeiters.*
  *Flaubert, Joyce and Beckett:
    The Stoic Comedians.*
  Joyce's Voices.
DANILO KIŠ, *The Attic.*
  Garden, Ashes.
  The Lute and the Scars
  Psalm 44.
  A Tomb for Boris Davidovich.
ANITA KONKKA, *A Fool's Paradise.*
GEORGE KONRÁD, *The City Builder.*
TADEUSZ KONWICKI, *A Minor Apocalypse.*
  The Polish Complex.
MENIS KOUMANDAREAS, *Koula.*
ELAINE KRAF, *The Princess of 72nd Street.*
JIM KRUSOE, *Iceland.*
AYŞE KULIN, *Farewell: A Mansion in
    Occupied Istanbul.*
EWA KURYLUK, *Century 21.*
EMILIO LASCANO TEGUI, *On Elegance
    While Sleeping.*
ERIC LAURRENT, *Do Not Touch.*
HERVÉ LE TELLIER, *The Sextine Chapel.*
  *A Thousand Pearls (for a Thousand
    Pennies)*
VIOLETTE LEDUC, *La Bâtarde.*
EDOUARD LEVÉ, *Autoportrait.*
  Suicide.
MARIO LEVI, *Istanbul Was a Fairy Tale.*
SUZANNE JILL LEVINE, *The Subversive
    Scribe: Translating Latin
    American Fiction.*
DEBORAH LEVY, *Billy and Girl.*
  *Pillow Talk in Europe and Other
    Places.*
JOSÉ LEZAMA LIMA, *Paradiso.*
ROSA LIKSOM, *Dark Paradise.*
OSMAN LINS, *Avalovara.*
  The Queen of the Prisons of Greece.
ALF MAC LOCHLAINN,
  The Corpus in the Library.
  Out of Focus.
RON LOEWINSOHN, *Magnetic Field(s).*
MINA LOY, *Stories and Essays of Mina Loy.*
BRIAN LYNCH, *The Winner of Sorrow.*
D. KEITH MANO, *Take Five.*
MICHELINE AHARONIAN MARCOM,
  The Mirror in the Well.
BEN MARCUS,
  The Age of Wire and String.

FOR A FULL LIST OF PUBLICATIONS, VISIT:
www.dalkeyarchive.com

SELECTED DALKEY ARCHIVE TITLES

WALLACE MARKFIELD,
Teitlebaum's Window.
To an Early Grave.
DAVID MARKSON, Reader's Block.
Springer's Progress.
Wittgenstein's Mistress.
CAROLE MASO, AVA.
LADISLAV MATEJKA AND KRYSTYNA
POMORSKA, EDS.,
Readings in Russian Poetics:
Formalist and Structuralist Views.
HARRY MATHEWS,
The Case of the Persevering Maltese:
Collected Essays.
Cigarettes.
The Conversions.
The Human Country: New and
Collected Stories.
The Journalist.
My Life in CIA.
Singular Pleasures.
The Sinking of the Odradek
Stadium.
Tlooth.
20 Lines a Day.
JOSEPH MCELROY,
Night Soul and Other Stories.
THOMAS MCGONIGLE,
Going to Patchogue.
ROBERT L. MCLAUGHLIN, ED., Innovations:
An Anthology of Modern &
Contemporary Fiction.
ABDELWAHAB MEDDEB, Talismano.
GERHARD MEIER, Isle of the Dead.
HERMAN MELVILLE, The Confidence-Man.
AMANDA MICHALOPOULOU, I'd Like.
STEVEN MILLHAUSER, The Barnum Museum.
In the Penny Arcade.
RALPH J. MILLS, JR., Essays on Poetry.
MOMUS, The Book of Jokes.
CHRISTINE MONTALBETTI, The Origin of Man.
Western.
OLIVE MOORE, Spleen.
NICHOLAS MOSLEY, Accident.
Assassins.
Catastrophe Practice.
Children of Darkness and Light.
Experience and Religion.
A Garden of Trees.
God's Hazard.
The Hesperides Tree.
Hopeful Monsters.
Imago Bird.
Impossible Object.
Inventing God.
Judith.
Look at the Dark.
Natalie Natalia.
Paradoxes of Peace.
Serpent.
Time at War.
The Uses of Slime Mould:
Essays of Four Decades.
WARREN MOTTE,
Fables of the Novel: French Fiction
since 1990.
Fiction Now: The French Novel in
the 21st Century.
Oulipo: A Primer of Potential
Literature.
GERALD MURNANE, Barley Patch.
Inland.

YVES NAVARRE, Our Share of Time.
Sweet Tooth.
DOROTHY NELSON, In Night's City.
Tar and Feathers.
ESHKOL NEVO, Homesick.
WILFRIDO D. NOLLEDO, But for the Lovers.
FLANN O'BRIEN, At Swim-Two-Birds.
At War.
The Best of Myles.
The Dalkey Archive.
Further Cuttings.
The Hard Life.
The Poor Mouth.
The Third Policeman.
CLAUDE OLLIER, The Mise-en-Scène.
Wert and the Life Without End.
GIOVANNI ORELLI, Walaschek's Dream.
PATRIK OUŘEDNÍK, Europeana.
The Opportune Moment, 1855.
BORIS PAHOR, Necropolis.
FERNANDO DEL PASO, News from the Empire.
Palinuro of Mexico.
ROBERT PINGET, The Inquisitory.
Mahu or The Material.
Trio.
A. G. PORTA, The No World Concerto.
MANUEL PUIG, Betrayed by Rita Hayworth.
The Buenos Aires Affair.
Heartbreak Tango.
RAYMOND QUENEAU, The Last Days.
Odile.
Pierrot Mon Ami.
Saint Glinglin.
ANN QUIN, Berg.
Passages.
Three.
Tripticks.
ISHMAEL REED, The Free-Lance Pallbearers.
The Last Days of Louisiana Red.
Ishmael Reed: The Plays.
Juice!
Reckless Eyeballing.
The Terrible Threes.
The Terrible Twos.
Yellow Back Radio Broke-Down.
JASIA REICHARDT, 15 Journeys Warsaw
to London.
NOËLLE REVAZ, With the Animals.
JOÃO UBALDO RIBEIRO, House of the
Fortunate Buddhas.
JEAN RICARDOU, Place Names.
RAINER MARIA RILKE, The Notebooks of
Malte Laurids Brigge.
JULIÁN RÍOS, The House of Ulysses.
Larva: A Midsummer Night's Babel.
Poundemonium.
Procession of Shadows.
AUGUSTO ROA BASTOS, I the Supreme.
DANIËL ROBBERECHTS, Arriving in Avignon.
JEAN ROLIN, The Explosion of the
Radiator Hose.
OLIVIER ROLIN, Hotel Crystal.
ALIX CLEO ROUBAUD, Alix's Journal.
JACQUES ROUBAUD, The Form of a
City Changes Faster, Alas, Than
the Human Heart.
The Great Fire of London.
Hortense in Exile.
Hortense Is Abducted.
The Loop.
Mathematics:
The Plurality of Worlds of Lewis.

FOR A FULL LIST OF PUBLICATIONS, VISIT:
www.dalkeyarchive.com

SELECTED DALKEY ARCHIVE TITLES

FOR A FULL LIST OF PUBLICATIONS, VISIT:
www.dalkeyarchive.com